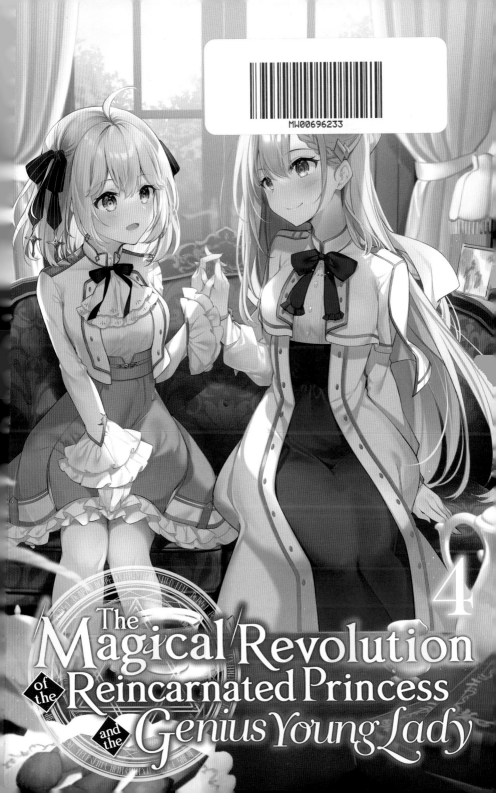

4

The Magical Revolution
of the Reincarnated Princess
and the Genius Young Lady

"Good morning, Anis. Thank you for dinner last night. It was a real treat."

Euphyllia Fez Palettia

Daughter of Duke Magenta. She set out to ascend the throne one day in Anisphia's stead and was named Second Princess.

"Ugh... You should respect your elders...!"

Anisphia Wynn Palettia
First Princess of the Kingdom of Palettia. Thanks to Euphyllia's assistance, she's been making strides in her research.

Lainie Cyan

Daughter of a baron and now a maid at the detached palace. A vampire with the power of enchantment.

Ilia Coral

Personal maid to Anisphia.
Has watched over her since
Anisphia was a little girl.

"Lainie...
would you
like *me*
to help?"

"Honor alone isn't enough. I want to give you so much more. I want to experience everything with you, Euphie."

"Anis...
am I
worthy
of your
honor?"

CONTENTS

Author
Piero Karasu

Illustration
Yuri Kisaragi

The Magical Revolution
of the Reincarnated Princess
and the Genius Young Lady

4 Piero Karasu

Illustration by Yuri Kisaragi

YEN ON
NEW YORK

The Magical Revolution of the Reincarnated Princess and the Genius Young Lady 4

Piero Karasu

Translation by Haydn Trowell
Cover art by Yuri Kisaragi

TENSEI OJO TO TENSAI REIJO NO MAHO KAKUMEI Vol.4
© Piero Karasu, Yuri Kisaragi 2021
First published in Japan in 2021 by KADOKAWA CORPORATION, Tokyo. English translation rights arranged with KADOKAWA CORPORATION, Tokyo through TUTTLE-MORI AGENCY, INC., Tokyo.

Yen On
150 West 30th Street, 19th Floor
New York, NY 10001

Visit us at yenpress.com | facebook.com/yenpress | twitter.com/yenpress
yenpress.tumblr.com | instagram.com/yenpress

First Yen On Edition: April 2023
Edited by Yen On Editorial: Rachel Mimms, Anna Powers
Designed by Yen Press Design: Wendy Chan

Yen On is an imprint of Yen Press, LLC.
The Yen On name and logo are trademarks of Yen Press, LLC.

Library of Congress Cataloging-in-Publication Data
Names: Karasu, Piero, author. | Kisaragi, Yuri, illustrator. | Trowell, Haydn, translator.
Title: The magical revolution of the reincarnated princess and the genius young lady / Piero Karasu ; illustration by Yuri Kisaragi ; translation by Haydn Trowell.
Other titles: Tensei ojo to tensai reijo no maho kakumei. English
Description: First Yen On edition. | New York, NY : Yen On, 2022.
Identifiers: LCCN 2021060085 | ISBN 9781975337803 (v. 1 ; trade paperback) |
    ISBN 9781975337827 (v. 2 ; trade paperback) | ISBN 9781975337841 (v. 3 ; trade paperback) |
    ISBN 9781975351656 (v. 4 ; trade paperback)
Subjects: CYAC: Magic—Fiction. | Princesses—Fiction. | Reincarnation—Fiction. | LCGFT: Fantasy. |
    Light novels.
Classification: LCC PZ7.1.K3626 Mag 2022 | DDC [Fic]—dc23
LC record available at https://lccn.loc.gov/2021060085

ISBNs: 978-1-9753-5165-6 (paperback)
        978-1-9753-5166-3 (ebook)

10 9 8 7 6 5 4 3 2

TPA

Printed in South Korea

The Magical Revolution of the Reincarnated Princess and the Genius Young Lady 4

The Story So Far

Princess Anisphia yearns for magic and yet cannot use it. After rescuing Euphyllia, a gifted prodigy, from the commotion of her annulled betrothal, the two young ladies set out on new beginnings. Together, they thwart Prince Algard's plot to usurp the kingdom, leaving Anisphia next in line for the throne. Eager to see her friend continue her beloved research, Euphyllia enters into a spirit covenant and declares her ambition to ascend the throne.

Characters

Tilty Claret
Daughter of a marquis—and a researcher of curses.

Algard Von Palettia
Anis's younger brother. Presently exiled to the frontier.

Orphans Il Palettia
King of the Kingdom of Palettia. Anis's father.

Sylphine Maise Palettia
Queen formerly responsible for the kingdom's diplomacy.
Anis's mother.

Grantz Magenta
Duke. Euphie's father and Orphans's right-hand man.

Halphys Nebels
One of Anisphia's research assistants. Daughter of a viscount.

Gark Lampe
One of Anisphia's research assistants.
An apprentice at the Royal Guard.

Piero Karasu
Illustration by Yuri Kisaragi

OPENING

I woke up feeling profoundly listless.

My mind still hazy, I sensed something warm near me and found myself reaching out to it.

It was such a comforting sensation, a mellow mood seemingly pulling me back into my dreams.

"Euphie…"

"Good morning, Anis."

The moment I heard her voice, I snapped awake all at once. The figure before me—the person I was reaching out for—was Euphie. Realizing that I was clutching her hand, I hurried to let go.

But she stopped me, holding me in an embrace from the front. I gasped for breath as I felt her body heat, smelled her scent washing over me.

"Let…go…!"

"Hee-hee… It doesn't take much before you start sulking, Anis." She chuckled under her breath as though she somehow found this amusing, before pressing her forehead against mine.

I gently headbutted her and forced myself upright.

My vision wavered slightly at the sudden change. Staring across at me in a sitting position, Euphie sat up straight, too.

"Good morning, Anis. Thank you for dinner last night. It was a real treat."

She seemed particularly cheerful this morning. I pursed my lips. My cheeks must have been bright red; I could feel them burning hotter by the second.

Since Euphie had become a spirit covenantor, we now had more opportunities to sleep by one another's side—for the sake of these so-called *meals*. We called them meals, although she was actually consuming my magical energy.

Spirit covenantors were essentially spirits in the form of a human vessel—and spirits relied on magical energy for sustenance.

They also needed normal food to maintain their bodies, but Euphie required magical energy more than anything. That was practically instinctive for her at this point.

The most convenient option to provide her with this energy was for us to remain in close physical proximity. That's why we now had so many more opportunities to sleep together.

I was fine with offering her my magical energy. The problem was that I was always left feeling so languid the next morning, and Euphie would act like a cute little imp, huddling close to me to absorb my energy, or else she would fawn over me and try to trick me!

"Ugh... You should respect your elders...!"

"Are you *still* saying that?"

Her exasperated smile only added to my vexation. I scrunched up my face in annoyance, but she must have found this amusing, as she poked my cheek with her finger.

"Stop it."

"Don't sulk, Anis."

"I'm not sulking."

Was this what it meant to be in love, this feeling of absolute weakness? She seemed to be toying with my feelings an awful lot lately.

I mean, I wanted to fawn all over her, too, but when she took my magical energy, it always left my head feeling dazed and stuffy—and that was when she would make her move. I didn't hate it or anything, but it was embarrassing and kind of frustrating.

"Hmm... Well, fine. Morning, Euphie."

"Yes."

Euphie was always in a good mood the morning after taking in fresh magical energy. She smiled at me as she looked me over. Sensing the emotions lurking in the depths of her eyes, I felt my chest tighten with nerves.

Watching her now, I was getting a little nostalgic for the old, confused Euphie whom I had first brought to live with me here. Before I knew it, she had completely morphed into this brazen, mischievous little demon.

Close to four months had passed since she had been adopted into the royal family as the kingdom's Second Princess. These bittersweet days, so blissful that they made me restless, were by now completely routine.

As the two of us messed about, I heard a knock at the door. It was Ilia.

"Lady Anisphia, Lady Euphyllia," she called from the hallway. "Good morning."

"Is it time already? Then let's get up, Anis. At this rate, we'll miss breakfast," Euphie urged, holding out her hand.

With a resigned shrug, I accepted her hand in my own.

And so began another day.

* * *

"Good morning, Lady Anis, Lady Euphyllia."

"Morning, Lainie."

After getting dressed and heading for the dining room, we found Lainie briskly hurrying about getting ready for the day. She'd settled into her role as a maid perfectly and had proven herself remarkably dependable.

The delicious aroma made my stomach rumble. I was always hungrier than usual after giving Euphie my magical energy, so I ate a little more than everyone else.

No one spoke during the meal, and we passed the time in silence. I was the last to finish eating, and that was when we finally started chatting lightly among ourselves—our usual custom.

"Thanks for preparing breakfast," I said. "I think I'll take it easy for a little bit today before heading out."

"If you would refrain from staying up all night and get out of bed on time, you would be doing me and Lainie a huge favor," Ilia said. "Or perhaps we should let Lady Euphyllia rouse you in the mornings from now on?"

"I don't mind...," Euphie replied.

"Well, *I* do," I objected, "and the answer is no!"

I'd been woken up by Euphie once before, only to find her engaging in a little *sampling*. I wouldn't be able to maintain my magical energy or physical health if she was allowed to do *that* every day.

"...If you would only let yourself get used to it..."

"Ilia, why do you seem so disappointed?"

"I'm not. I certainly wasn't thinking that you're acting rather worn out."

"You're saying it out loud, though!"

I—I wasn't worn out! I was just trying to practice some moderation! Right—moderation was important!

Ilia must have been reading my mind; her warm gaze turned inscrutable. Euphie's teasing—and, well, Ilia's too—had become relentless ever since we'd fallen in love with each other. It was more than a little irritating.

Euphie took this all in stride with an innocent look, but Lainie's gaze was filled with sympathy. Her reaction made me almost feel like breaking down into tears then and there.

"You're the detached palace's resident healer, Lainie...," I said. "Don't ever change..."

"Yes...," she breathed softly, her expression unreadable.

Well, that was enough tomfoolery for one morning. It was time to get ready for the day ahead.

My current task was preparing for the introduction of magical tools.

Thanks to my accomplishments so far, many more people were willing to hear me out and consider the value of my magical tools. I was genuinely happy with this development, but it also meant I had to give real thought to this challenge so that I could communicate my ideas most effectively.

Compared to the old days, my thinking really had undergone a transformation. Before, I had been so desperate in my pursuit for acceptance— and then, one day, I had given up. In a way, it was convenient not having to chase after people's understanding. That must have been what had led society to labeling me "Princess Peculiar."

I had been pretending to be something that I wasn't, trying to protect anyone from reaching my heart. In retrospect, I didn't have the strength or composure to get away with it. It was thanks to everyone around me now that I was finally able to take a good, hard look at myself.

That was why the present moment was so deeply precious to me. And because I was so happy, I wanted to do *something* to make this feeling last even longer, grow even more intense.

"I guess we should get going, then," I murmured.

"Yes. Have a nice day, Lady Anisphia."

"Take care, Lady Anis!"

I left Ilia and Lainie to clean up after breakfast and set out from the detached palace with Euphie by my side.

She tugged at my hand, staring my way expectantly. After a moment's hesitation, I leaned in to give her a peck on the cheek.

"…I—I'll see you later."

"You're still not used to this, are you? In that case—"

"No!"

I hurriedly reached out to stop her as Euphie tried to kiss me on the lips. She stared back at me for a long moment, then shook her head.

"You've been snacking too much recently, so no more."

"…Are you sure?"

"I'm sure!"

Honestly, she'd become so obnoxious lately. Given the chance, she wouldn't hesitate to suck the magical energy right out of me!

She must have taken a liking to the taste and was clearly adapting to life as a spirit covenantor. Still, that wasn't to say that I *didn't* want to be nibbled on at every opportunity. My heart was crazy for her.

"…It's fine, isn't it? Just a kiss. I mean, if it was nighttime…"

"Night is night! Morning is morning! Yes, you're a princess now, Euphie! You ought to be able to switch between different roles!"

Come back to me, my perfect, model student Euphie! Quickly, before I forget my sense of shame.

"I suppose it can't be helped. I'll see you later then," she said, withdrawing.

I let out a deep sigh. To think, back when we met, I was the one who had her wrapped around my little finger. What was I supposed to make of this unsettling feeling?

As my thoughts continued to lead me astray, Euphie leaned in, catching me off guard. She wrapped her arms around mine to hold me steady, then brought her mouth close to my ear as she whispered, "If you *treat* me tonight, maybe I'll be able to cut back on the snacks. I'll always be waiting for you."

"Euphie!" I found myself exclaiming.

My face was so hot that it must have been bright red.

Maybe her *snacking* was because she wasn't taking in enough magical energy to fully satisfy her cravings. But that could only mean that she needed more intimacy, and while I didn't *not* want that, this wasn't the right kind of place to have this conversation—and even then, it wasn't exactly an easy discussion to have…!

"I'm kidding."

With those words, Euphie effortlessly untangled our arms and fixed me with a smile like a child who'd just pulled off a prank. After lifting a finger to her lips, she turned around in an unmistakably buoyant mood.

She seemed so happy that I could practically see musical notes coming out of her as she left.

I hung my head as deep as it could go. "She acts so serious…but she's so, so awfully mischievous at the same time…!"

She'd been far too earnest for that to be a joke. Was this what it meant to see a different side of someone after getting close?

As it happened, Euphie's temperament was one quality that she had in common with her father, Duke Grantz. I had realized this for myself only after bringing her here to work with me, though.

On top of that, Euphie's mother, Nerschell, was similarly capable of hiding her true thoughts behind the faintest of smiles. Euphie had certainly inherited some strange traits.

"…What more does she want with me?" I wondered aloud before giving my head a good shake to clear my thoughts.

I had work to do—I couldn't afford to slack off forever! With that private reprimand, I slapped myself on the cheeks to return to the task at hand.

CHAPTER 1
Meeting a New Friend

"Good morning, Duke Grantz."

"Good morning, Princess Anisphia."

Recently, I had found myself working with the duke on a regular basis, and this morning, too, I paid a visit to his now-familiar office in the royal palace.

The duke served as chancellor of the realm, and to put it bluntly, his workload was extraordinary. Since we'd started working with him, I had come to realize exactly how my father and the duke's excessive duties could drive one crazy. In a sense, it was no wonder that the two of them had so little time to dedicate to their families.

That being said, apparently those responsibilities had become somewhat easier to manage now that my mother had retired from her role as a diplomat and was presently assisting my father. His work was overly harsh and exploitative, and to be honest, I did worry about his health.

I understood that it was a little late for apologies, but I was reminded yet again just how much trouble and heartache I had put him through. Those unrelenting stresses were probably why he looked a full decade older than his actual age. I truly was sorry.

…On the other hand, I couldn't help being astounded by how Duke Grantz hadn't seemed to age at all, and he never seemed in the slightest bit tired. Were the Magentas actually a family of superhumans like Euphie?

"So, Duke Grantz," I began, "what do we have on the agenda today? Another one of my lectures?"

"No, there are no lectures scheduled for today, nor any inspection plans, either," he answered. "I've already seen to it that the various knightly orders be informed of developments through your previous ones."

"Ah, right. So what am I supposed to do, then?"

"The most pressing tasks have been taken care of, so your main work now will be in the selection and testing of magical tools as we introduce them to society. If you have any ideas for new inventions, please feel free to prioritize them, too."

"Can I?"

"At present, there is no need for you to take any urgent actions. Several knights of the Royal Guard are currently undertaking trials of your magical tools, but that will still take some time to complete. You will, of course, be required to carefully examine the results, but that task still lies ahead of us."

"Ah...I see."

"I'm quite sure that there will be more work to be done following their full dissemination, but for now, the priority is on development. If you are concerned about political affairs, those are the responsibility of Princess Euphyllia."

I couldn't help but stare back guardedly as Duke Grantz referred to his own daughter by her royal title.

Even since Euphie had been adopted into the royal family, severing all ties to the House of Magenta, Duke Grantz had taken to calling her either *Her Highness* or *Princess Euphyllia.*

But there was nothing that I could say about it if they decided to establish their new relationship as one of lord and vassal rather than child and parent. I was impressed—amazed, even—and at the same time, I couldn't help but feel somewhat guilty.

Then again, I *had* seen Euphie sticking her tongue out at Duke Grantz on more than one occasion since becoming a princess, so perhaps theirs was now a somewhat healthier bond. When she had first come to join me in the detached palace, she seemed to think that her father's word was absolute.

That being the case, maybe what they had now—a little friendly competition in which they occasionally butted heads—was better for the both of them. Still, it sounded like the duke was giving Euphie a fair number of difficult problems to take care of, so I *did* want to do something to help. Why? Because she would only end up taking her pent-up stress out on me later, of course!

"That's all I have to say for our future plans, but I would like to take this opportunity to add some fresh faces to your staff."

"Huh? You mean you want me to take someone on as an assistant?"

"Yes. Considering our goal of further popularizing magical tools, it would, I believe, be wise to ensure that we have more individuals equipped with a full understanding of how they work. To that end, I would like to recommend two names. Both will also serve as personal protection, so they will be seconded from the Royal Guard."

"From the Royal Guard...? Ah, so they'll be my assistants and escorts, but you also want them to one day teach others how to use magical tools?"

"The Royal Guard is the first to formally receive your direct instruction, Princess Anisphia, but we will one day need an independent group of individuals who specialize in teaching."

"I want to *develop* more tools, though, so I can't spend all my time teaching others how to use them."

In recent weeks, I had been hard at work preparing for the wider dissemination of magical tools, so I hadn't had much time to focus on creating new inventions. That being the case, it was only natural that we would need more such individuals to serve as instructors into the future. If these new staff could help accomplish that, then I would be more than happy to take them on.

"I have already called them here, in fact. May I ask them in to meet you?"

"Yes, please."

As I gave my consent, Duke Grantz rang the bell to call them in. After a short pause, the two individuals entered the room.

The first was a girl with clear blue eyes and light brown hair tied back and braided—reminiscent of a committee chairwoman. Perhaps her glasses were partly responsible for that impression.

The other was a well-trained young man with a striking physique. He had short black hair and eyes so narrow that it was difficult to tell whether they were open or closed. Looking closely, I could see that his irises were dark brown; his overall countenance vaguely reminded me of a Buddha from my past life.

I had never seen the girl before, but I recognized the man with the Buddha-like face as a knight. As I observed them inquisitively, the two bowed deeply before me.

"It's a pleasure to meet you, Princess Anisphia. My name is Halphys Nebels; I'm the daughter of Viscount Nebels."

"And I'm Gark Lampe, an apprentice in the Royal Guard!"

The girl who introduced herself as Halphys greeted me with the graciousness expected of a lady of the nobility, while the young man, Gark, appeared slightly nervous.

I pressed a fist into my free hand when I realized his name sounded familiar.

"I thought I recognized you, Garkie!"

I had met him once during my activities as an adventurer, while participating in a joint field exercise incorporating both knights and adventurers for Viscount Lampe. At the time, Gark had been an apprentice in his family's own group of knights.

"*Garkie...?* I—I'm honored you remember me..."

"How many years has it been? Wait—you're with the Royal Guard now? What happened to your family's band of knights?"

"I decided to join the Royal Guard to try to broaden my horizons. I'm honored to have been chosen as Your Highness's personal attendant."

"Huh. This is a bit of a surprise."

"Rekindling old acquaintances is a lovely thing, Princess Anisphia," the duke interrupted, "but perhaps I should explain everything first?"

"Ah. Sorry, Duke Grantz. Please."

I had let myself get distracted upon seeing a familiar face, derailing the whole conversation. I mentally scolded myself and sat up straight.

"Very well. I would like you to keep Halphys Nebels and Gark Lampe by your side. Halphys is a civilian apprentice within the Royal Guard, and Gark is a squire. Both show great promise. When selecting them, I took into account their personal compatibility with Your Highness, so I hope there won't be any inconvenience."

"I'll serve you to the best of my ability, Your Highness," Halphys said, turning enthusiastically my way.

Her eyes were dazzling, as though faced with the object of long admiration—her gaze was so powerful that I almost fell back in my chair. I had never seen an aristocrat's daughter look at me with such ardor before.

"My turn, then. I'm Anisphia Wynn Palettia. I look forward to working with you."

I reached out to shake hands with the two. Both of them looked somewhat apprehensive.

With the introductions out of the way, Duke Grantz continued. "Well then, Princess Anisphia, that's all I had to say. I shall send a messenger to inform you when your next appointment is decided. Until then, feel free to spend your time as you wish."

"I understand. In that case, I'd like to get to know these two better today. If anything else comes up, let me know."

Duke Grantz nodded his assent, and with that, I left his office with my two new attendants in tow.

"Well, let's go someplace quiet to talk."

"As you will, Your Highness," Halphys answered, still looking somewhat tense.

I hoped that she would relax and start acting normal around me before too long. Garkie seemed a little nervous as well, but at least he wasn't as anxious as Halphys.

Wondering where in the royal palace would be best for us to talk, I eventually decided to ask a maid, who recommended the courtyard. I asked her to make some tea, and then we made our way there.

Palace staff often used the courtyard to relax. But within its grounds, there was also a particularly impressive section reserved almost exclusively for the royal family.

Back when my mother was a diplomat, she would come home from time to time and bring me here for a good lecturing. I recalled this memory with a faraway look in my eyes. Halphys and Garkie, neither of whom would normally have any opportunity to set foot within these grounds, seemed awestruck.

"...Why don't we sit down?" I suggested.

"Th-thank you," Garkie responded, kindly pulling out some chairs.

Finally, once he, too, had taken his seat, the tea arrived. I was glad to see that the maid had brought some small cakes to accompany the drinks.

"Let's start over, then, I guess. What should we talk about first?"

"This is our first meeting, but I take it you've met Gark before?" Halphys asked.

"I worked with Viscount Lampe's knights back when I was an adventurer. Are you two acquainted?"

"Gark and I have known each other since a little before he joined the knights. He was in the same class as my fiancé at the Aristocratic Academy."

"Ah, so it's only you and I meeting for the first time? In that case, you can let your hair down a little. I don't like being too formal, and I want to get along with you both as best we can."

"Um, er..."

"I agree; don't lean on formality," Gark teased her. "This is just who Halphys is, you know?"

"G-Gark!"

Halphys seemed more than a little flustered by Gark's behavior—he had all but told her to get on with it.

Watching the two, I felt a grin forming on my face.

"Compared to how *you* were when we first met, Garkie, she isn't being rude at all," I commented.

"Th-there's no need to dig up the past, Lady Anisphia!"

"Right, what was it you said again?" I wondered aloud. *"If you're here for a bit of fun, Princess, go home! This is no place for games!"*

As I delved through my memories and repeated his words back verbatim, I saw Garkie visibly convulse, covering his face with trembling hands to hide his shame.

"And then I basically sent *you* home. This is *much* better than that!"

"Really, I—I know I made a mistake back then! Please, don't dig it all up again!" he moaned, almost in tears.

Such fond memories. In those days, I hadn't properly established myself as an adventurer yet, and Garkie had pounced on me when he had realized my true identity.

"It was just meant to be a joint exercise, but we ended up getting attacked by monsters, and it descended into an outright melee. Garkie was the only squire who was able to hold his own, so I remembered him well."

"…You've been really amazing since then, too, Lady Anisphia. I always knew you would change the realm someday, but you've turned out to be even more incredible than I expected," Garkie said as he scratched the back of his head.

The affection and respect in his tone of voice were so noticeable that I felt a slight tickle work its way up my back.

"That's right. I've long wanted to serve you, Princess Anisphia, and now that wish has finally come true."

"You too, Halphys? *Have* we met before…?"

"Not directly. If we did, it would only be because I'm the same age as Princess Euphyllia and Miss Lainie."

"Oh? So you were a classmate of theirs?"

"We were just in the same year, that's all. I've never interacted with Princess Euphyllia; we're from different factions, you see. As for Miss Lainie, well, what with the situation at the time…"

"Ah, right. Lainie… Well, that couldn't be helped…"

At the Aristocratic Academy, Lainie had been surrounded by troublesome characters, my brother Allie included, so it was understandable that Halphys wouldn't have interacted with her.

"By *different factions*, do you mean the group affiliated with the Ministry of the Arcane?"

"Yes. That's the one."

"In that case, are you sure you want to throw your lot in with me? Really?"

"Even though we're affiliated with the Ministry of the Arcane, my family is neutral. From Your Highness's perspective, you might think of us as opportunists…"

"Ah, so that's it…"

Did she mean the group within the Ministry of the Arcane that hadn't been overly concerned with me and my magicology research?

It was the extremists within the ministry who had hated me, and they were by far the largest faction. At the same time, there had also been a minority who considered my research worthy of deeper consideration.

The remaining members of the ministry had remained neutral, waiting to see which way the wind would blow. And so the ministry had been divided 6:3:1, between the extremists, those who had yet to take a formal position, and those in favor of tolerance.

"The announcement of your flying magical tool was a major impetus. But I wanted to get to know you even before that."

"Before the announcement? Why?"

"I'm ashamed to admit it…but my magic skills aren't very good. My fiancé works for the Ministry of the Arcane, but I wasn't good enough for that. I became a civil servant connected to the Royal Guard instead," Halphys confided, her expression darkening slightly.

"Basically, the Ministry of the Arcane and the Royal Guard aren't exactly on good terms…," Garkie murmured.

I paled a little at this turn of the conversation.

The Ministry of the Arcane was composed of the kingdom's elites, but it was rare for them to deal with any of the incidents that occurred throughout the realm directly. From the point of view of the various knightly orders, the ministry was obsessed with politics and completely unconcerned with the realities of the world.

Many people within the ministry, on the other hand, viewed those knights as whiners who had failed to reach the same lofty heights as themselves, so the two groups were at odds in a whole range of respects.

The knights in the Royal Guard tended to be more open-minded, but the bureaucratic nobles in the royal capital certainly weren't popular among more local knightly orders.

On top of that, there were also lingering resentments from the coup d'état during my father's youth. That was probably why I had been kept at a distance from politics from a young age. In any case, the two issues were deeply intertwined.

"There's no way around it, seeing as I don't have any real talent for magic. But there have been times when I've even doubted the spirits themselves because of it all."

"...Halphys, that's—"

"I know. That practically disqualifies me as a noble of the Kingdom of Palettia. But even so, I couldn't get rid of those thoughts," she said, her expression pained and forlorn. "I read the magic textbooks again and again, along with all the reference materials. I changed my daily routine, praying more fervently than I ever had before, making sure not to miss even a single day. But nothing changed. Every day was a trial. I couldn't bear it anymore, so I confided in my parents and teachers. But they all said the same thing: that my prayers weren't sincere enough. That so long as I harbored distrust in my heart, I would never be able to improve my magic skills..."

I found myself sympathizing with Halphys's confession to an almost painful degree. I had been wrestling with the same grief and hardship for a great many years.

For the nobility in the Kingdom of Palettia, the ability to wield magic was valued more highly than anything. I knew all too well how hard it was to live in such a society when you were unable to develop that potential for yourself.

And I knew how it felt to be unable to change that cursed reality, no matter how much you wished and prayed for it.

"I want to change. If at all possible, I wish I could be like you, even if only a little bit. That day, when I saw Your Highness flying through the sky, I couldn't dream for anything else. That's why I'm so overjoyed to have been given this opportunity." Halphys's gloomy expression had turned to one of fierce determination.

My heart trembled under the heat of her gaze. If I hadn't held my composure, I might have even spilled a tear or two. Here was someone else who had experienced the same suffering that I had, and she was still trying to move forward and make her dreams come true.

All this only helped to bolster my determination. I wanted to help her. I couldn't afford to neglect her passions.

"Studying magicology won't necessarily improve your magic skills, and I'm not sure whether it will help you achieve what you really want. But even so, I'll do everything I can to support you, Halphys. I'll offer you my strength, and I'd like you to offer me yours in turn."

"Yes, thank you so much!" she responded forcefully.

That smile of hers was a truly steadfast one; I couldn't help smiling back.

"I'm not really good at magic, either, and I might not be as fervent as Halphys here, but I'm going to take this seriously. So here's to working for you, Lady Anisphia!"

"Yep, yep. It's good to have you, too, Garkie."

"…I've been meaning to say something for a while now, but can't you just call me by my name?!"

"Eh…? But it's easier just calling you *Garkie*, isn't it?"

"Am I imagining things, or are you treating me with a little bit of contempt? I'm imagining it, right? Right, Princess Anisphia?!" he protested loudly.

Halphys broke into a weak smile at this exchange, and her soft laughter echoed through the courtyard.

* * *

That evening, I sat down to talk to Euphie in my room after eating dinner and taking a bath.

She had been kept quite busy ever since she had been adopted into the royal family as a princess. Lately, we had less and less time to spend together, so she at least tried to make up for that by meeting for a night-time chat. Still...

"So I'm sure Halphys and Garkie will learn a whole lot by my side, and they'll both be instrumental in spreading the word of magicology through society."

"...Oh?"

"...Euphyllia?"

I realized I was addressing her somewhat formally. I mean, she was staring at me so expressionlessly that I couldn't read her emotions in the slightest. D-did I say something to upset her?!

"Don't you think you're being a little overenthusiastic about this Halphys girl?"

"Eh? No, um, er...Euphyllia?"

"*I'm* not thinking that, you know?"

"But you're saying it?"

"I'm *not* thinking it."

"...You're jealous?"

"What do you think, Anis?"

At that moment, something my troublesome friend Tilty had said to me echoed in the back of my mind: *"Euphyllia might* look *composed, but she's harboring a deep jealousy inside her. So be careful."*

Indeed, now that we'd become so close, I could feel her pulling away from me a bit again.

A chill ran down my spine. Uneasy, I glanced back at Euphie, still giving me a smile that I knew was anything but happy.

"Um, no, no, you're misunderstanding..."

"...I'm joking."

With that, the frigid atmosphere dissipated, and Euphie let out her usual laugh. Had it really just been a joke? I stared across at her in suspicion.

"She's the daughter of Viscount Nebels, yes? So she was in the same class as me at the Aristocratic Academy. I know her fiancé, then."

"You do?"

"He's the one at the Ministry of the Arcane who was particularly kind to me. The youngest son of Count Antti."

"Ah, Count Antti? That makes sense."

The Antti family was a central pillar of the neutral block at the Ministry of the Arcane.

They ranked among the most powerful of the neutral families, and I knew for a fact that both the family head and his eldest son worked at the ministry.

I had even exchanged a few brief words with both of them, and as far as I recalled, neither was the kind of person who could easily be misled or swayed.

"Since the extremist faction lost most of its influence, the neutral group is now the biggest force in the Ministry of the Arcane. It's hard to convince them to give their full approval, though, because they're not our friends or allies."

"Neither friend nor foe, huh?"

That would indeed be a problem. If they were allies, we could trust them to be flexible, and if they were enemies, we could come up with ways to break their opposition. But when trying to bring a fence-sitter into your camp, you needed a good reason to convince them to join up.

"Even when others take things too far, the neutralists remain indifferent," Euphie noted. "As far as they're concerned, it's none of their business, so they don't want to get involved... Having to deal with the ministry has just served to remind me that they're a little *too* traditional."

"Sticking to tradition means that they won't be willing to accept change..."

"That's exactly right. There's a complete lack of support there for reform."

For her to complain like this, Euphie's attempts to assert control over the ministry must not have been progressing particularly well.

Yet as a spirit covenantor, Euphie was essentially the flag bearer for the wealth of traditions inherited by the Kingdom of Palettia; it was her

hope and goal to spread the word of magicology and magical tools to usher in a new age.

But the Ministry of the Arcane was reluctant to accept the changes that we were both trying to bring out. They weren't directly hostile, but it was precisely their lukewarm reception that was proving troubling.

Refusing to accept new ways of thinking, not wanting to change the way things had been up till now—they were practically refusing to shed their biases. And their reluctance could prove fatal to the reforms that Euphie hoped to carry out.

"Honestly, I'd do just about anything if I could get them on board," she observed.

"Yeah... But we don't want to force them, right?"

"No. I chose this path because I want to bring change to the realm. But I don't want to force others down the same road against their will...," she said with a deep sigh, her face betraying her exhaustion.

"Let's go to bed, Euphie," I suggested.

"Anis?"

"So long as you don't take all of it, I'll let you have a little of my magical energy."

It would leave me drained and exhausted if she kept taking my energy day after day, but I figured that I could afford to spoil her a little bit here. Compared to my work, Euphie's was significantly more difficult.

I went to bed first, with Euphie following shortly after. No sooner had she lain down than she drew close to me, burying her face in my chest.

She exhaled deeply, settling in.

"There's no need to rush," I said, patting her on the head. "Let's think about it together—how we can persuade everyone at the Ministry of the Arcane."

"...They hate you there, don't they?" Euphie sulked.

For once, she was acting her age. It was so cute.

"It's because they don't like me that I might be able to come up with ideas *you* wouldn't have thought of, Euphie. Anyway, you don't have to shoulder it all alone. Ilia and Lainie will have your back."

"…Yes, of course. I know that."

She lifted her head—which until that moment had been buried in my chest—and brought her lips up to mine for a kiss. Then, after a few pecks, she shifted her mouth to my neck.

I felt a calming warmth as she rested her lips there, the resulting heat almost enough to make me shiver.

A soft, balmy sensation took root at the back of my head while she drained my magical energy. I kept running my fingers through her silky hair, which brought me so much comfort.

"…Actually, I wasn't being entirely truthful before," Euphie whispered as she moved back.

"Huh?"

"I *was* jealous of Miss Halphys."

"…I don't see her that way, you know?"

"I know. That wasn't what I meant. I was your assistant once, too; that's all."

Still hugging me, Euphie glanced upward. Her rose-colored eyes wavered for a moment, her sullen expression perfectly appropriate for her age—and to be completely honest, unbelievably cute.

"We made the Arc-en-Ciel and several other magical tools together… But when I think about everything that lies ahead of us…well, it makes me feel a little lonely, you know?"

"Euphie…"

"I know this is necessary, to secure the future we both want. But…," she murmured, pursing her lips and burying her face in my chest again, leaning into me oh-so-sweetly. "But what I really want is to stay by your side, without any obligations or responsibilities. I want to be the number one person in your life… That's why I got jealous when you were talking about Halphys so enthusiastically."

"Hmmm…!"

What was she saying, this cute little devil?!

"You *are* my number one, Euphie. Even when we're apart, you're always the most important person in my life. You support my dreams the most, and I love you more than anyone else."

I rested a hand on her cheek and leaned in to kiss her on the forehead as she glanced up.

I couldn't help feeling glad that she was jealous over me. That was enough to tell me how special I was to her.

That made me want to dote on her even further. I loved her more than anyone and wanted nothing more than to be together with her.

"We chose this path so we *can* be together, forever, and so everyone else would recognize that. Don't worry. Our paths will always be as one," I said, patting her on the back as though comforting a child.

"I love you, Anis," Euphie told me, drawing closer.

"I love you, too."

She leaned in for a kiss—longer this time than a short peck. We closed our eyes, savoring each other's presence. It was so irresistibly lovely and joyous, this moment between us.

I wanted to know even greater happiness, and I wanted to share that feeling with Euphie, too. And if at all possible, I wanted more people to feel the same.

From the very bottom of my heart, I wanted to spread that joy as far as possible, with everyone.

"…Halphys has a fiancé, so she's off-limits, you realize?"

"Hold on. I'm not interested in everyone, you know?! I'm not that unprincipled!"

"You say that, Anis, but you never know. You could end up stealing someone's heart without even realizing it. You're not exactly trustworthy in that respect…"

"Huh…?"

Just as I wondered whether I was perhaps overthinking all this, Euphie's eyes began to glaze over.

Uh-oh, I thought, but it was too late. She held on to me tightly, all but declaring that she wouldn't let go.

"So just don't, please…?" she told me.

"I wouldn't try anything, though…!"

"If you think you can get away with doing it unawares, I'll have to teach you the error of your ways, you realize?"

"Um, Euphie? I said you could only have a snack today!"

"Right, snacks are just fine. And I'll have as many as I like."

With a smug grin, she kissed me on the lips to cease any further argument, a hand reaching out to hold me by the back of my head.

This many snacks basically adds up to a full meal!

I wasn't able to point this out to her until the next morning, though.

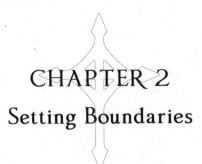

CHAPTER 2
Setting Boundaries

"Good morning, Princess Anisphia."

"Morning!"

"Welcome to the detached palace, Halphys, Garkie."

The very next day after the two of them had been formally assigned as my attendants, I invited them to my villa at the detached palace.

With an eye to the future, I realized that it would be necessary for them to learn more about the study of magicology and to broaden their knowledge. Seeing as Duke Grantz had no other tasks for me, I invited the two of them for a visit to see my magical tools for themselves.

"I'll introduce you. Ilia's here, and Lainie. They're maids here at the detached palace, serving Euphie and me. Halphys, I think you've seen Lainie before, right?"

"My name is Ilia. It's a pleasure to meet you."

"And I'm Lainie. If you need anything, please let us know."

As I introduced them, Ilia and Lainie both bowed in polite unison. I felt a surge of pride rising up in my chest to see how Lainie could now stand tall by Ilia's side.

"I... Ah, no. I'm Gark Lampe, of the Royal Guard." Though briefly letting his true colors show, Gark soon corrected himself, greeting the pair in the manner expected of a knight.

"Halphys Nebels, also of the Royal Guard," Halphys added courteously, before turning her gaze to Lainie. "We were in the same class at the Aristocratic Academy, but I'm afraid we never had an opportunity to speak with one another, Miss Lainie."

"…Not at all. Considering my behavior at the time, it's only natural that we didn't get to know each other. I must apologize."

"There's no need, really. I just thought it would be nice if we could get along, seeing as we have a lot in common. I'm sure you had to put up with a lot of hardship back then. I'm happy to see you're doing well now."

"Thank you, Lady Halphys." Lainie bowed her head, looking somewhat embarrassed.

She still seemed a little awkward, but I hoped that the two of them could set off on the right foot.

After introducing Ilia and Lainie, I led Halphys and Garkie to my research lab.

"So this is Your Highness's laboratory…!" Halphys exclaimed, her voice rich with excitement as her eyes darted around the room.

Gark, by her side, was similarly taking it all in, his gaze brimming with curiosity. "This is where Your Highness researched magicology and built your magical tools."

"Many of them I actually ordered from workshops in the castle town, but everything that I could do myself, I assembled here. Now that I'm supplying the Royal Guard, I've got to outsource a lot of things, though."

I asked the two of them to sit down before brewing them each a cup of tea using the most popular of my magical tools here at the detached palace—my Thermal Pot. Halphys was a little flustered to have her tea prepared by the princess, but I urged her not to bother herself with such minutiae.

"This is nice," Garkie remarked. "It would be useful for expeditions and outdoor activities."

"I always kept one handy when I was working as an adventurer."

"It's hard work starting a fire when you're out and about, especially when you're on duty during the rainy season," he added, staring at the Thermal Pot with admiration.

Halphys nodded along to his remarks.

Among all my magical tools, the Thermal Pot was one of the easiest to use and had a wide range of applications, so it tended to make the best starting point for explanations.

"The patterns in the design of the pot were made using paints made from spirit stones and other raw materials, and they work in the same way as a chant or invocation."

"I see. So it takes considerable craftsmanship to make them. Wouldn't it be possible to make a lot of jobs for craftsmen mass-producing them, then?" Halphys asked.

"I would love that, but they use fire-type spirit stones, so that could affect households that use them for fireplaces and igniters. If we start making too many, I'm afraid there won't be enough materials. I don't want the prices to jump."

"In other words, the widespread adoption of magical tools could affect the consumption of spirit stones that people use in everyday life…"

"They're convenient, so I'm not afraid they won't sell. I'm more worried about them *over*selling. They'll end up changing the way everyone has lived their lives. Until now, given my position, I couldn't take responsibility for their success or failure. That's one of the reasons I've chosen not to promote them."

The ideas behind my magical tools were rooted in the knowledge that I had inherited from my past life—knowledge of a world that had flourished without magic, a world filled with conveniences beyond compare with the current standard of living here.

Magical tools derived from such ideas could have a very stimulating effect on this world. That had been obvious to me ever since I had first used them.

There was my Thermal Pot, capable of keeping water at a set temperature without a fire, and then my Mana Blade, a highly portable weapon that could be used for self-defense. And of course, numerous flying magical tools that could render conventional means of transportation obsolete.

Just thinking back on the tools I had already produced, I recognized that the impact they could have on the world was already too great.

"That just goes to show how amazing your work really is!" Garkie exclaimed.

"No, not really... I mean... Maybe...?"

He was exaggerating a little there. He had to be. Was it me, or did his response imply that I would be causing a new commotion every time?

"Really? Every single one of your magical tools is something that utterly confounds conventional wisdom, though, isn't it?"

"That's why I've been reluctant to promote them too hard, and why I asked the Royal Guard to do preliminary testing, Garkie."

"I can't tell if you're bold or prudent, Lady Anisphia..."

"When you're bold, be bold! When you're prudent, be prudent! Take the best of both worlds!"

"That's one way to put it!" Garkie said with a broad grin.

I gave a hearty laugh. Considering the difference in our social positions, this exchange was probably far from appropriate, but I did prefer this kind of banter. Halphys, on the other hand, let out an exasperated sigh.

"Let's talk seriously here for a moment," I continued. "I've neglected social and political matters up till now, so while I'm pretty familiar with the lives of the common folk, I'm not well informed of the affairs of the nobility. And it's the nobles who actually run the political sphere, right? Even if I knew what the people wanted, that doesn't mean much if you can't convince those at the top."

"Ah... That's true," Halphys responded. Her expression was unreadable.

Still, I could guess what it meant. I was on bad terms with the bureaucratic nobles who actually governed the realm.

Most bureaucratic families held their high-ranking titles either because they worked directly at the Ministry of the Arcane or because they were otherwise associated with it in one way or another.

Those high-ranking families tended to produce the kingdom's elites, and they were also usually more religiously devoted to the worship of spirits. That was because high titles and the size of one's house were often linked to financial power, which in turn led to a greater emphasis on education.

The more extensive one's education, the deeper their understanding of spiritualism, too. And the more devoted a family was to those beliefs, the less respectable *I* would be in their eyes.

After all, I was a princess unable to use magic, one who hadn't even fulfilled her duties as royalty.

"I don't exactly think things are *good* the way they are, but it's not like I can do anything about them. However, Duke Grantz's faction has my back."

"The militarist faction…mostly composed of local nobles and those with low-ranking titles."

"I think the fact that Duke Grantz gave me the opportunity to do my lectures on magicology is partly so I can get to meet those nobles. If they're regional nobles, they might actually end up feeling closer to me, or that we have a connection of some kind."

"You used to be an adventurer, too, right?" Gark remarked. "You were a great help to my family."

"No, no, no. I owe you. So I guess I could ask for the people's approval or encouragement. But at the end of the day, I won't be able to get anywhere without agreement from the top."

As it happened, I *was* in a position where I could go directly to my father, and I had already shared my magical tools with those in my direct vicinity. Because of that, I already had received permission to some extent—or rather, my actions had been overlooked to a certain degree.

I wouldn't be able to do that from now on. My father, Duke Grantz, and Euphie, aspiring to become queen, all wanted to see my magical tools adopted throughout the realm.

But there was no way that I could share them with the whole kingdom alone. So I needed others to lend me their strength. But at the same time, I didn't want to have to keep relying on others. What I wanted were relationships that were mutually advantageous.

"Yep, we're probably going to need something a little easier to share with people."

"You mean a different kind of magical tool?" Halphys asked.

"Yep. The ones I've already made are definitely convenient, but people won't understand how helpful they are until they actually use them for themselves."

"Ah. The Thermal Pot and Mana Blade might suffer from that problem, yes."

"I'm aware that my knowledge is extremely biased in areas, so I'm hoping that you, a proper noblewoman's daughter, will be able to give me some advice."

"If I can be of service, I'll do my best to help, Your Highness," she answered, raising her hand to her chest with a determined look.

She really did strike a dependable pose there. Here in the detached palace, none of us were particularly familiar with what the aristocracy considered common sense. Euphie was from a ducal family, Lainie was a former commoner, and Ilia had left her family home long ago.

This might not have been the best way of phrasing it, but the opinions of the two individuals before me, belonging to the middle or even lower ranks of the nobility, would prove immensely valuable. As far as I was concerned, it was only natural that magical tools could help improve the things that people were already used to, but it was also important to use them to fill in the gaps, to bring new experiences to their lives.

"Ultimately, we're missing a trump card to help convince everyone at the top…"

"A persuasive trump card…"

"In the end, the only course of action I'm good at is developing magical tools. But even if the tools I've made now are things that the common people might want, they aren't the kind of thing *nobles* want."

"I'm sure there must be plenty of knights and adventurers out there who would like their own Thermal Pot and Mana Blade, but those already good at magic probably wouldn't see much need for them…," Gark observed.

"There are still a lot of people who question magical tools. But I think the demonstration of your flying tools is starting to change opinions somewhat…," Halphys added, raising a finger to her mouth and furrowing her brow in thought.

But it wasn't long before her tone of voice turned grave. "No, even with that, it might still be difficult to bring them around… Flying magical tools are exciting and make for good publicity, but they're too innovative an idea."

"Huh? You mean…they're not good enough?" Garkie asked curiously.

Halphys, looking almost daunted, shook her head. "Flying magical tools have already shown their value, so that's fine. But if we were to make Thermal Pots a common household object, the role of fire-type spirit stones would have to change dramatically. Princess Anisphia, you said earlier that you decided not to introduce them too fast because you couldn't take responsibility for them—but if they do take off, and if a problem arises down the line, who do you think will have to deal with it?"

"Who…? You mean, Lady Anisphia? Because she made them?" Garkie asked.

"Of course. When it comes to fixing magical tools, responsibility will fall on Her Highness. To put it plainly, that will prove to be a loss."

"A loss?"

"Magical tools may become widespread, but something will still go wrong at some point of the process. When it does, the realm will have to make a choice, whether to go back to the way things were before, or whether to introduce improved versions of the tools. And when the governing authorities take action of that kind, people and money will be involved. Gark, are you following me so far?"

"A-ah, right. I understand that much."

"If there is a guarantee of success, everyone will invest in it. And flying magical tools have proven to be just such a success. But because flight is still such a new concept, it isn't clear what the potential gains and losses might be."

"…O-oh?" Garkie murmured, smoke all but billowing out from his head, his mind no doubt overloaded.

"…Are you all right there?"

I let out a small chuckle, before adding a few thoughts of my own: "This is just an example, but let's say we managed to increase adoption of flying magical tools. If there were a lot of accidents—losses, as you say—what would happen next? Would it be right to keep on introducing them? That's what you mean, Halphys, isn't it?"

"…Right. So if we're going to introduce them, we'll need to do something about that, huh?" Garkie murmured.

"That, however, would cost a lot of money," Halphys noted. "It isn't fully clear what the losses would be if flying magical tools fail, so for the time being, we can forget about testing the waters too far. Worst-case scenario, if it fails, we can simply halt development."

"There's no precedent for flying magical tools. But whether it's a Thermal Pot or a Mana Blade, if there's a possibility of replacing or competing with something that already exists, people will be reluctant to try it. Because they'll see a clear loss if it fails, right?" I asked.

"That's because some people might lose out due to the change. For instance, if everyone wanted Mana Blades, it would make it next to impossible to sell ordinary swords, which would put the blacksmiths in a bit of a bind, don't you think?" Halphys pointed out.

"…That would definitely be a problem."

"But if an issue popped up with the Mana Blades, it wouldn't be easy for society to go back to regular swords. I mean, a lot of blacksmiths would have already gone out of business, and there wouldn't be enough of them. That's a very real possibility."

"…That *would* be real headache…," Garkie groaned, furrowing his brow in thought after listening to our explanation. Then, head tilted to one side, he threw out a new question: "So basically… Huh? People are reluctant to accept change because they don't want to risk losing something else?"

"It's probably more accurate to say they don't want to take any risks that could result in a loss, I guess? So it isn't really magical tools that have been accepted at the moment, but only flying magical tools."

"That's only natural when your own career is at stake. It's often said that those at the top are expected to shoulder these kinds of responsibilities... although that doesn't work when people only take responsibility when they feel like it."

"But in that case, nothing would ever change. Only successful ideas would ever become popular, right? But if Thermal Pots and the like became commonplace, wouldn't regular people want to make use of them after seeing how beneficial they can be?"

"...Indeed. But I think it's precisely because the Kingdom of Palettia *hasn't* changed that we're now faced with so many problems."

"...Ah, I see what you mean. So that's it..." Garkie, convinced, crossed his arms as he nodded to himself.

For her part, Halphys let out a tired sigh.

In fact, the realm had remained unchanged for generations. But if you were to ask me whether this situation could continue forever, I would have to say no. The coup d'état at the start of my father's reign, along with the turmoil that ensued when my brother, Allie, broke off his engagement with Euphie, was proof enough of that.

"If we were to try to change the status quo, there would seem to be broadly two main ways to do it," Halphys continued. "Either we change things slowly and patiently, or you gamble on taking a plunge."

"So would spreading the word of magical tools be a gamble?"

"If things continue as they have been, yes."

If Euphie hadn't become a royal princess, I would have been left with no choice but to take that risk. And in that case, the realm might well have descended into chaos. Even now, that was still a very real possibility.

So the task that lay ahead was to patiently convince those around me of the merits of my inventions. And yet I didn't have the necessary cards to pull that off. *That* was the problem.

"I'm stuck trying to think of new ideas, though…," I muttered.

"…In that case, how about we browse the archives at the Ministry of the Arcane?" Halphys suggested.

"The ministry's archives?"

"Yes. Reports from all over the kingdom are stored there. Looking over past records, I think we should be able to work out what sort of magical tools would be most suitable for broader introduction."

"Hmm… That's true, I guess… The archives, huh…?"

I had indeed visited the place when I was little, but not since my falling-out with the ministry. It had basically become hostile territory.

But Halphys was right. What I lacked now was knowledge and ideas, so it was only natural to seek out fresh information to fill those gaps. The only issue was that said information was under the jurisdiction of the Ministry of the Arcane, with which I had a bit of a history.

"…You don't think it will work?" Halphys asked.

"…It's been this way for a long time. But I suppose there's no use dwelling on the past."

The situation had changed, so I couldn't let past roadblocks stand in my way.

And it wasn't like we were talking about marching in there by force. It would only be to look at some documents. We weren't going to do anything wrong.

"In that case, why don't we see what's available? What should we investigate, though…? We could maybe start with the amount of spirit stones collected in each area. What they're used for, how frequently, their distribution by territory… We probably won't be able to do it all in one go, though. First things first, we'll need to gather all the materials and information…"

"Um, Princess Anisphia?" Garkie interjected.

"Hmm? What is it, Garkie? You look a little pale."

"Er, does that mean I'll be helping you?" he asked nervously.

"Eh?"

"Come on, let's all do our best!" I said, fixing him with a broad grin. "Halphys, Garkie!"

"Whoa, it's like my nightmares from back at the academy are coming to life! A whole mountain of assignments!" Garkie cried.

"Ha-ha-ha. I've never been to the academy, so I wouldn't know," I commented.

And so I set off for the Ministry of the Arcane, dragging a reluctant Garkie along with me. I might have heard Halphys let out an exasperated sigh as she chased after us, but I was happy to pretend that it was just my imagination!

* * *

The archives at the Ministry of the Arcane were legitimately enormous. It was no exaggeration to say that the entirety of the Kingdom of Palettia's accumulated history up to the present moment had been preserved within its walls.

Part of the archives was open to the public much like a library, but that was only a small section. From what I had learned, important documents and books that had been designated as restricted were kept in an area accessible only by ministry staff.

When I set foot inside the public area, I was met with a flurry of rude glances. A murmur rippled through the hall, while people rushed fearfully out of our path. Even from a distance, I could hear them all whispering to each other, clearly annoyed by my presence.

"...I've got a bad feeling about this," Garkie said in a low voice.

"Well, there's nothing to be done about it."

He sounded almost sullen. I had expected this kind of response, but I still wasn't happy experiencing it.

"First of all, should we check to see if the materials we're looking for are actually in this section? Let's ask the librarian."

"I'll check," Halphys offered. "Please wait a moment, Princess Anisphia."

"Would you? We'll stay here. I'd probably make a nuisance of myself if I keep moving around obliviously."

"Very well. I'll be right back." With that, Halphys hurried off to the reception counter.

Garkie and I, on the other hand, were left to wait. There was no respite from the people watching us from a distance, and now that we had come to a stop, I could easily hear the susurrus of whispers all around us.

"Yep. It's pretty clear I'm not welcome here. It almost makes me want to laugh out loud."

"...It does, doesn't it?"

"Don't *you* get awkward on me now, Garkie. I know it's hard, but it's against the rules to get into any arguments in here."

"I know that much. It's just..."

"...Just what?"

"...It just made me realize how badly they treat you. It's disgusting..."

He clicked his tongue and looked about ready to lash out. His dark brown eyes, normally narrowed into a thin line, were now slightly open, fixing the room with a glare.

The thought of him getting angry for my sake made me a little uneasy. I gave him a pat on the back, trying to feign indifference.

"I don't mind. I certainly haven't been perfect, either."

"...But doesn't it hurt, this sort of treatment? The way they're looking at you—it's so harsh."

"Really, it's all in your head!"

This exchange must have quelled Garkie's rage somewhat, as the tension slowly subsided.

Almost as soon as he had calmed down, I heard a familiar voice say, "Anis? What are you doing here?"

"Euphie."

Indeed, Euphie was coming right this way, clutching a book in her hands. Behind her was a young man with dark brown hair and a quiet and serious aura.

"I was thinking of digging up some research materials... Ah, Euphie. This is Garkie, one of my new attendants I told you about earlier."

"Can't you at least introduce me with my real name?! Ahem! Gark Lampe, at your service."

"Anis has told me all about you. I'm sure she must be bossing you around quite a lot, but please do take good care of her," Euphie responded with a gentle smile.

Despite this, Garkie still seemed somewhat nervous and restless.

Meanwhile, the man behind Euphie let out a small chuckle at Garkie's distress.

"...Don't laugh, Marion," Garkie spat, glowering at this individual.

"Sorry, Gark. I was just worried you might be getting too uptight after finally realizing your dreams. Don't take it personally."

"Shut up! You don't need to say all that out loud!"

"...Garkie, do you two know each other?" I asked.

"My apologies for not having introduced myself, Princess Anisphia. My name is Marion Antti."

"Marion Antti... Count Antti's son? So *you're* Halphys's fiancé?"

"Yes. She's taking good care of me," he said with a modest bow, still clutching the book in his arms.

Halphys's fiancé... I couldn't help but feel that they looked like they could run a committee together.

"Gark and I were in the same class at the Aristocratic Academy."

"Ah, so that's your connection. I brought Halphys with me, too, but I asked her to check with the librarian about finding some materials..."

"...Oh?"

Euphie breathed a melancholy sigh, while Marion wore an ambiguous smile that could easily have been mistaken for a wry grin. I frowned at the two of them.

"...Maybe it would have been better if I hadn't come here?" I asked.

Euphie seemed troubled for a moment, as though unsure how to explain. After a short pause, she seemed on the cusp of saying something when a new voice called out.

"Excuse me, Princess Anisphia? May I have a moment?"

"...Lang?"

Catching me off guard was an unexpected face—Lang Voltaire, one of the so-called *elites* at the Ministry of the Arcane, a bespectacled intellectual who had a history of remonstrating with me.

As usual, he looked exceedingly anxious. No—upon closer inspection, his expression was at least twenty percent grimmer than normal.

I expected him to offer another one of his caustic remarks—but then I spotted a bewildered Halphys standing beside him. It didn't take long for her to notice Marion and offer him a light bow.

Taking in the situation from the sidelines, I turned to Lang and asked, "Can I help you?"

"I've heard about the reason for your visit today, so I've come to offer some explanation. Perhaps we should discuss the details in a private room? I'm afraid that people are watching us here."

"...Indeed."

We couldn't possibly have a proper conversation with so many people watching on so disrespectfully. I had no idea what Lang wanted to talk about, but I didn't exactly have the liberty of not hearing him out.

"In that case, this way, if you will. Please excuse us, Princess Euphyllia."

"...Yes. Thank you, Lang."

"Your kind words are wasted on me. Keep up the good work, Marion."

Euphie seemed a little put out at having Lang take charge of the situation, and she left with Marion by her side.

Before leaving, I noticed Marion pat Halphys gently on the shoulder, while she nodded with a smile. That sight was enough to mend my spirits somewhat as I turned back to Lang.

Lang offered them both a final nod before leading us from the main area to one of the reception rooms, calling out to a maid on the way, instructing her to prepare tea.

"Please, take a seat," he urged once we were inside. "We should be able to offer you tea momentarily."

"We didn't come here to drink...," I pointed out. "Will this conversation take long?"

"No, it shouldn't. I wouldn't want to waste your time by beating around the bush. Shall we cut to the chase before the tea is brought in?"

"Please."

"Thank you... Firstly, you're aware that part of the library in the royal palace is open to the public, I assume? It provides studying and learning opportunities to aristocratic children who aren't old enough to attend the Aristocratic Academy, as well as palace staff."

"That's general knowledge, even to me. What about it?"

Indeed, among the maids and attendants working at the royal palace, there were those who continued to reside at their family homes while working as apprentices.

Such apprenticeships were intended partly to provide financial relief measures for those who wanted to attend the Aristocratic Academy but lacked the necessary funds to afford tuition, and to enable struggling students the opportunity to engage in independent study.

Over time, the number of people who took advantage of such arrangements had increased, leading to the establishment of the library as it existed today. I myself used to go there when I was little, and it was particularly popular among book-loving nobles and young children.

"Yes. So there are no restrictions whatsoever should Your Highness wish to visit the library to peruse those books. I should point out, however, that the materials that you have requested are not kept in the public areas."

"I see... You didn't bring me here just to tell me that, I assume?"

"No. It was simply necessary to establish the premise of this conversation."

"I hope you're not getting full of yourself, Lang. What do you want from me?"

"Then let's get straight to the point. I'm here to ask you to please refrain from accessing the archives in person for a while," he said, never breaking his gaze on me.

I narrowed my eyes back at him—but it was Halphys and Garkie whose reactions were even more pronounced.

"Lord Lang! What are you talking about?!"

"Why shouldn't Princess Anisphia use the archives? You haven't explained anything! What kind of authority allows you to ask that?!"

"Calm down, you two, please," I said. Next, I turned my attention back to Lang. "Is there something going on here? Well, I suppose it was inevitable. It's hard to think how my relationship with the Ministry of the Arcane could be any worse. Is that it?"

"I'd like to clear up any misunderstandings. I don't have the authority to prevent you from accessing the archives, Your Highness. I'm only asking you not to."

"So you've got no ability to compel me? But why don't you want me to access them? What's the reason? I won't insist as forcefully as Garkie did, but I want to hear what you have to say, Lang," I said, staring probingly his way.

Lang fell silent for a long moment, before finally breathing a heavy sigh. "The Ministry of the Arcane is presently without a director due to the revelations of Count Chartreuse's crimes. The former director is presently overseeing the ministry in his place, but I'm afraid I can't quite say that he's in command, so to speak."

"I've heard rumors along those lines. But what does that have to do with me using the archives?"

"The ministry is reeling at the moment. From the news of the director's corruption, the impact of your demonstrations of your flying magical tools, Princess Euphyllia's adoption into the royal family…and most surprising of all, the truth about spirit covenants," Lang said, looking me square in the eye as he shared his various thoughts.

True, Euphie had shared with the nobility the true nature of spirit covenants—contracts that transformed a person by becoming one with the spirit that dwelled inside them.

Their body would become immortal, their mind and soul shifting in nature. Over time, their attachment to their physical form would fade away, until eventually they abandoned it, becoming what in the past had been termed a great spirit, or an Elemental.

This revelation, so major that it shook the very foundations of the kingdom's spiritualist beliefs, had been met by the nobility with immense shock and confusion. Among them, those nobles deeply associated with the Ministry of the Arcane had no doubt been particularly affected.

They had worshipped spirits as incarnations of the absolute—but the targets of their reverence had, in the end, been nothing more than transformed humans. The truth was still rippling through society as though someone had just thrown a boulder into a huge lake.

The ensuing chaos was to be expected. And of course, simply withholding this information from the public was an option under consideration. But it was Euphie herself, who had already become a spirit covenantor, who insisted on revealing the truth.

Entering into a spirit covenant was by no means an easy task. Even with these revelations, it was unlikely that another spirit covenantor would be found anytime soon. Rather, Euphie believed it wouldn't do to leave the traditional spiritualistic beliefs in place when people had no grasp of what they truly entailed.

I understood that Euphie, who had entered into the covenant unawares, didn't want to be placed on a pedestal.

However, this revelation was a powerful drug. Which was why Euphie herself had come to the Ministry of the Arcane to take the reins and guide us out of this turmoil.

All of this was to say that I knew without needing to be told that the ministry was on tenterhooks—but from the way that Lang looked, perhaps the situation was even more precarious than I had assumed.

At this point of the conversation, everyone kept their mouths firmly shut as a heavy silence filled the room. I really did feel bad for the maid when she arrived with the tea.

After taking a sip of my cup to clear my thoughts, I turned back to Lang.

"I understand the situation, but I still don't see what it has to do with asking me to refrain from using the archives."

"At present, a great many individuals who work at the ministry are feeling heavy pressure. They are anxious about the future, distrustful now that the foundations of their faith have been called into question, and fearful that they may even lose their own positions…and everything else as well. All the result of Your Highness's demonstration, and Princess Euphyllia's announcement."

"…Heavy pressure?" I repeated, scratching my cheek as I mulled over those words.

Yet what they prompted inside me were cold, unsympathetic thoughts.

"Considering how poorly you lot have been treating me, it sounds like now that my position has improved, you're all worried about your own."

"If that's how you see it, I can't leap to our defense. But that is why I would prefer that you don't personally get involved with the ministry at present. I'm sure you're aware of the dangers of prodding a wounded beast."

"…Is everyone here really so on edge?"

"Let me just say that even Princess Euphyllia is having difficulty getting a handle of it all."

I let out a deep sigh and rubbed my brow. That answer was enough for me to understand just how bad the situation was.

"I have a few thoughts of my own about the current situation," Lang added. "I have no idea what exactly the outcome would be if any unnecessary stresses build on top of the current pressures. Some individuals are so run down that there's really no telling what they might do. Please understand—I don't want to see any of our people run amok."

"…But isn't that all your problem to handle?" Garkie retorted before I could get a word in. "It doesn't have anything to do with Princess Anisphia, does it? And I'm sure plenty of other people come here wanting to access information. Why should only Princess Anisphia be denied access?" He was flaring at Lang, no longer able to stand this treatment.

"G-Gark!" Halphys cried, trying to restrain him before he could reach out to grab Lang.

Lang glanced Gark's way, then slowly rose from his seat. Finally, after approaching me, he knelt down on the floor and offered me a deep bow.

"As you say, I know this is an unreasonable request. Ultimately—Your Highness is under no obligation to comply. But I ask of you, please refrain from involving yourself with the Ministry of the Arcane at the present time. If you need any materials, I will send someone to deliver them to you at the detached palace. I would also ask that you send any additional requests through this messenger and abstain from visiting the archives in person."

Not even Gark seemed able to respond to this. He sat there biting his lip and looking conflicted.

"...Lang, I understand. I don't want to see the ministry descend into chaos, either. So I'm willing to go along here."

"...Thank you."

"But I can't *accept* it... *You* are the ones who have been mistreating *me* all this time."

"...I can't deny that."

"At the same time, I didn't behave in a way that you all found acceptable, either. So let's strike a compromise here. I don't want to make things any worse between us. That isn't my wish. If you're willing to help me get the information I want, then let's end this discussion here. Raise your head."

With that instruction, Lang slowly stood up. I didn't know him well enough to guess what was going on behind that emotionless mien, and now wasn't the time to try to find out.

"Halphys told you what I'm looking for, right? It would probably be too much to send me everything, so the librarian's recommendations will be enough. If anything is missing, I'll have you send more."

"Understood."

"Then I'll leave you to it. Let's go, Halphys, Garkie."

The two nodded, the both of them looking vaguely troubled.

Before we left, I caught sight of Lang watching us. I probably shouldn't have said anything, but I couldn't help calling out, "Lang?"

"...What is it?"

"If *you* could enter into a spirit covenant, would you? Even if it meant giving up your humanity?"

He didn't respond, simply staring back at me in silence.

I didn't wait for him to speak up before continuing, "You don't have to answer me right away. It probably wouldn't have been a good sign if you had."

"...Princess Anisphia."

"Good. I'm sure that's the right kind of response. What you've believed in all this time isn't wrong. Those thoughts and wishes have protected the Kingdom of Palettia for generations. But I am sorry."

My heart faltered. It was screaming and breaking under the pain that I had overlooked for so long. Agony now made real. The innermost feelings that I had always wanted to give voice to.

"Even turning to faith and tradition, I couldn't use magic. Because I don't have a shred of magical talent. So I can't live in a world where people tell me to give up."

Was my voice trembling? I couldn't help wondering, but that didn't stop me from speaking my thoughts.

"No one acknowledged me. No one believed in me. It was like torture; I was abandoned, denigrated, treated as worthless. Maybe I should have just died. Maybe it would have been better for everyone if I had never been born."

My clenched fists were trembling. I exhaled to quiet my heart, beating so fast that it felt like it might explode. I didn't want to curse or harm this man. But still I couldn't stop. From the very bottom of my heart, all I wanted to do was scream.

All this time, all the things that I had been holding back—they were now seeping out. I knew full well that I was simply lashing out, venting my pent-up anger. But still there was so much that I had wanted to say to him, to all of them, for so long.

"After all this time, why are you acting afraid of me now? *You* denied *me*. If you had denied me to the very end, I wouldn't have to worry so much. It would have been easier if you had just put it all down to us not seeing eye to eye... So why now? Why are you telling me all this now?"

Lang had no answer. He continued to stare at me, without averting his gaze. This could well have been the first time he had looked me straight in the eyes. Up till now, no doubt he hadn't thought me worthy of looking upon directly.

"I know it's useless saying all this now. I know I need to overcome these doubts. Still, there's only much I can stand...Lang."

I fought to keep my voice as steady as possible, but even so, I couldn't stop it from trembling.

"How long do I have to put up with you all constantly rejecting me?"

Tell me. If you're going to reject me, then tell me. Don't just reject me. You don't need to understand *me. I don't know anything. I don't want to see it. I don't want to hear it. Any of it. I don't want to have to shoulder this weight anymore.*

My wounds, exposed by Euphie, still hurt. They were agonizing, but still I forced myself to lift my face and keep going. I was more than just these wounds. So I could keep looking forward.

"...I want to meet you all halfway. If we can't, then I'll have to fight you. But I hope it won't come to that. I'm sorry for taking this all out on you."

"...Not at all."

Those were Lang's only words.

And with that, I turned my back on him and left the reception room.

CHAPTER 3

Let's Build a New Magical Tool!

After being asked to leave the archives by Lang, the three of us made our way straight back to the detached palace. Garkie was making little effort to hide his displeasure, and Halphys watched on with concern.

I asked Ilia to prepare some tea so that we could all cool down. Once I'd told her everything that had happened, she frowned slightly.

"To think that such a thing could happen at the archives…"

"Yeah. It sounds like things over at the ministry aren't going as well as I thought."

"But it isn't fair that *you* can't use the library set aside for everyone to access, Lady Anis!" Lainie said with an indignant huff.

She had her own bone to pick with the Ministry of the Arcane, and this latest incident seemed to have upset her greatly.

For some reason, everyone around was even angrier about all this than I was, leaving me feeling like I simply didn't have the time to feel outraged.

"It is what it is. I think the ministry really is at its limit right now. I mean, they're having to deal with fresh knowledge that brings their whole worldview in question. Besides, I'm not looking for a fight, so I'll put up with it."

"…I don't want you to have to say you've got no choice, Lady Anis," Garkie whispered uncomfortably, his eyes slightly narrowed.

"Garkie?"

I thought that he must have calmed down, but it looked like his irritation and dissatisfaction had yet to fully subside.

"What you're trying to do is for the benefit of the whole kingdom. And you've already made a difference, as you demonstrated with your flying magical tool. Right? And what has the Ministry of the Arcane ever done for all the regional nobles? All those loudmouths care about is tradition and status. They're always looking down on people like us from the countryside, calling us rustics and whatnot. What right do *they* have to ask you to stay away?"

"I know what you mean, but if we get started down that path, there will be no end to it…"

"You *do* have a choice! You did everything you were supposed to do, Lady Anis! It's *them* who haven't! And yet it's *your* freedom that's restricted? I can't stand for it!"

Garkie, clenching his fists, looked even more frustrated than I was. Not sure how to respond to this display of indignation, I glanced around at the others for help. Lainie, however, seemed to agree with Garkie, while Ilia and Halphys didn't appear inclined to challenge anything that he had just said.

"…I came to the royal capital because I wanted to join the Royal Guard—and because I admire you, Lady Anis."

"Huh?"

"After losing to you, I felt so pitiful, so ashamed, especially when I saw you taking such an active role in the monster encounter during that training exercise. At first, I thought you were making fools of us all— but no. You were being perfectly serious. You couldn't even use magic, but you built your own magical tool instead and did your best to stand up for everyone by yourself. I couldn't live with myself after witnessing all that. So I joined the Royal Guard, hoping to serve at your side."

I stared back wide-eyed at this confession. Naturally, I *had* wondered why Garkie, who was poised to become the next leader of a regional knightly order, would choose instead to join the Royal Guard—but it had never occurred to me that this might be the reason.

"Anyone could use that magical sword, even if they weren't nobility. Just building such a device was impressive enough, but then you put in the time and effort to actually master wielding it, too. I don't think anyone else could be like you—not easily, that's for sure. But you showed me magnificent possibilities. *That's* why I want to support you, Lady Anis…" Garkie stopped there, his shoulders drooping as he lost his strength. "But *I* wasn't any help to you at all…"

"That's not true. Just hearing all this is encouraging by itself, really."

There were a lot of people who, like Garkie, were enthusiastic in their support for me. Euphie, Ilia, Lainie, my father, my mother, and many more who weren't always by my side—so many people who supported and believed in my dreams.

I was overjoyed to have met both Halphys and Garkie. They, too, were people with whom I wanted to march toward a bright new future— allies with whom I could chase the same dream.

"It's true I'm not exactly on good terms with the Ministry of the Arcane, and there are times when I don't really feel truly free. But that's also because I've neglected my relationship with them, too, so the blame goes both ways. That's why I want to start over. This time, I want all kinds of people to recognize me. But this isn't something that can be solved today or tomorrow, so let's just keep moving forward, one step at a time."

I couldn't claim that Lang's attitude was good, per se, but at the very least, it had been considerably better today than in the past.

Change was already happening. My task was to make sure that those changes weren't bad ones.

Everyone who had heard my words seemed to be dealing with them in their own way. That alone was enough.

Without a doubt, my voice had reached someone—and that realization alone gave me the strength to move forward.

My goal remained far off in the distance, but so long as I kept it within my sights, there was no need to hurry. It might feel good to run selfishly ahead until you exhausted yourself, but you risked collapsing along the way.

So instead, I would move forward hand in hand with everyone else, at a shared pace. Well, I might pull them along a little, maybe swing them around a bit—but all in good fun!

* * *

Sometime after Halphys and Garkie left for the day, Euphie returned to the detached palace.

As soon as she saw me, her expression turned apologetic.

"I'm really sorry about today, Anis," she called out tiredly. "I should have told you ahead of time."

"You mean about the archives?" I said as we entered the dining room. "I don't mind. I didn't think things were so tense at the ministry, so I ended up acting a little carelessly. And I should have consulted with you first, so we're both at fault."

Our routine had developed to a point where Euphie normally arrived home just as dinner was almost ready. After eating, she would go straight to take a bath and rest. That was the current rhythm of our lives. If she was ever going to be late, she would send a messenger to let us know in advance.

She was no doubt tired, so first things first, I let her eat. I had suggested as light a meal as possible tonight, and that seemed to have been the right call, as she swallowed it all down with gusto.

After eating, it was time for our usual chat. As was to be expected, the topic of conversation today was what had happened in the archives.

"I heard from Lang afterward. Apparently, he asked you to refrain from visiting the archives…"

"Yeah. There's no way around it, what with the way the ministry is right now. But they're almost treating me like a pest or something…"

"They must be very worried. Their spiritualistic beliefs are deeply entrenched. It will be a problem for me, too, if they don't change, though…"

"You don't think it's working out?" I asked.

Euphie arched an eyebrow at this. "I'm afraid not…," she said reluctantly after a short pause. "I've been trying to secure allies, but it's taking a long time to find people with the right mindset, and I haven't reached a proper starting point yet. Marion and Lang have both been very helpful, so it's not as if I haven't made any progress at all, but even so…"

"Marion I expected, but Lang, too?"

I was taken aback. I wouldn't have imagined someone with an attitude like his to have joined Euphie's cause.

"I can't say he's an *ally* exactly, but he isn't an enemy. I think he might actually be good enough to serve as the next director of the Ministry of the Arcane. He's still young, but if he can gain some more experience, I'm sure a lot of people will support him. In fact, from what I can tell, it's mostly thanks to his efforts that the ministry has been able to maintain a modicum of order during all this."

"You're willing to go that far…?"

"Yes. I would like to bring him to our side if possible… But while he isn't hostile, he isn't exactly friendly, either. We're basically just working together to keep the ministry from falling into chaos and disarray."

"Lang hates magicology… But I'm happy to hear he isn't too hostile at least."

It was true—we had argued so much in the past that it was difficult to call our relationship anything other than antagonistic. Perhaps in his own way, Lang had been reflecting on what existed between us.

Euphie, however, was rubbing her brow in frustration, seemingly vexed by the situation. While she could rely on him, she still couldn't consider him an ally.

Even here at the detached palace, it was rare to see her expressing such distress. Perhaps this, too, was the result of long exhaustion.

Just as I was about to suggest that she go and take an early rest, Lainie spoke up. "Lady Euphyllia, may I ask you something?"

"Lainie? What is it?"

"May I accompany you during your work at the ministry?"

All of us were surprised at this sudden proposal.

Euphie cocked her head. "What are you suggesting, Lainie?"

"You're having trouble working out who is on your side, aren't you? In that case, I thought maybe my abilities could help."

"Your abilities... You mean your vampire powers?"

Vampires were born from former humans and could blend in with society and conceal their true identities.

They possessed the power of attraction—enough to make others like them and to render them susceptible to the vampire's will.

Ever since she had developed the skill necessary to control her powers, Lainie had kept them consciously sealed away. I'm sure her inadvertent use of them in the past was, for her, a particularly bitter memory.

And so this suggestion came to us all as quite a surprise. But now that she had our attention, she caught her breath for a second before continuing, "Of course, I don't mean manipulating them with my powers of attraction."

"I don't expect anything like that from you, Lainie... But what *would* you use your vampire powers for?"

"I've been exploring other ways to use them, and I've recently realized that I can use them to sense people's emotions."

"Is that even possible?"

"I've been practicing using my powers, and I think I'm getting the hang of it. I'm able to read people's emotions by gauging their reactions when trying to work out what kind of dreams to show them...and I think I could use the same technique to find people who are favorable to you, Lady Euphyllia. That should help you to decide who to try to recruit, right?"

Euphie lifted a hand to her mouth, her expression turning serious as she pondered Lainie's suggestion.

It certainly did make sense—if she could read people's emotions, that would make narrowing down a list of potential allies so much easier.

What's more, I thought that it wouldn't do to make her engage in any spy-like activities. It really was a relief that she herself was committed to not abusing those powers.

However, it would be dangerous if anyone who didn't know her well enough was to learn of her vampire abilities. No matter how humanlike she might look and act, vampires were still considered monsters because of the magicite crystals within their bodies.

Plus, a vampire's powers could easily destroy entire countries, so it wasn't hard to imagine how many people would hate to just leave one be.

"...That sounds dangerous," Euphie retorted. "This is the Ministry of the Arcane we're talking about, and there might still be some extremists there who know the truth about you. Even if most of them have been purged and removed from power, it would be too optimistic to think they're all gone. And even if they don't know about you just yet, we don't want to accidentally tip them off."

"But if they were going to be suspicious, wouldn't that have already started a long time ago?" Lainie asked.

"I suppose that's true..."

While no one spoke about it anymore, few could have forgotten the fiasco that had ensued when Allie had called off his engagement.

Just because there was a new buzz going around didn't mean that the incident had been forgotten.

According to the public explanation, Lainie had been caught up right in the middle of it all simply as an innocent bystander.

The fact of the matter was that she had been ensnared by events out of her control—but would people actually believe that? It wasn't impossible that there would still be those monitoring her every movement.

"It's easy to reject this power. But you've taught me ways not to reject it," Lainie said, staring straight at Euphie, her eyes burning with determination as she placed a hand over her heart.

The two of them remained that way for a while. Eventually, Euphie let out a resigned sigh.

"...Very well. But if things start looking dangerous, I'll ask you to stop at once. All right?"

"Yes! Thank you!"

"I should be the one thanking you. Please lend me your strength, Lainie."

Euphie and Lainie, back to being true friends, exchanged smiles. The two had begun to develop a close bond ever since the incident, but I really was pleased to see how they had become so amicable.

But with Lainie accompanying Euphie, Ilia would be left alone here at the detached palace. I glanced toward her to see whether she would betray any sadness at seeing her adorable student go, but before I could crack a joke, she turned her gaze.

My breath caught in my throat. Ilia looked as composed as ever. But as she watched Euphie and Lainie smiling together, I realized she was actually only seeing Lainie.

Her eyes seemed to convey a hint of loneliness, but she quickly tilted her head to one side as though she herself couldn't understand precisely what she was feeling.

I fought to swallow the words on the verge of escaping my lips.

That was a close call...!

I raised a hand to my chest to calm my racing heart at this unexpected reaction. I had very nearly kicked a hornet's nest.

I've never seen Ilia react like this before...

Perhaps not even she fully understood her own feelings here. Ilia was often ignorant of her own emotional states, and she rarely articulated them.

She simply held everything in, acting as though nothing ever troubled her. That was how she had been trained.

I had no idea how exactly she felt about Lainie, only that she had been enchanted by her powers on at least one occasion.

But it wasn't like she had been subjected to those powers ever since, and I didn't get the impression that she had been acting out of the ordinary lately.

Then again, if she wasn't aware of it herself, there might not be any visible changes in her behavior. And of course, Ilia had always been somewhat modest when it came to asserting herself.

...Is this...? Is this what I think it is...?

It would probably be best, I realized, to keep an eye on her for a while. I only hoped that things didn't get too peculiar.

And so I was left racking my brain as a fresh wave of apprehension rolled in.

* * *

A few days after Lainie started accompanying Euphie to the Ministry of the Arcane, a messenger arrived at the detached palace while I was giving Halphys and Garkie a primer on the fundamentals of magicology.

Bringing the materials that I had requested from the ministry was Halphys's fiancé, Marion, and a second young man, his hair a dull golden color, his eyes dark brown, and his bearing vaguely playful and frivolous.

"Hi there, Princess Anisphia!" He greeted me with a friendly smile. "It's an honor to finally meet you. Oh, my apologies! My name is Miguel Graphite. Looking forward to working with you!"

"Ah…"

I was at a total loss as for how to respond to his buoyant exuberance. He wasn't even vaguely what I would have expected from someone who worked at the ministry.

"No, getting to meet *the* Princess Anisphia in the flesh—this has to be the work of the spirits themselves! It's almost too much!"

"Thank you…?"

"Miguel, you're bothering Her Highness. Please, restrain yourself."

While I struggled to formulate a response, it was Marion who came to my rescue. *Goodness gracious*, Miguel all but murmured as he waved a hand in front of his face.

"Ha-ha-ha! Ah, I'm sorry! I just couldn't contain my excitement! I've heard about you from Lang and everyone at the ministry! I hope you'll be so kind as to forgive us!"

"…You don't belong to the Ministry of the Arcane, Miguel. Don't apologize on our behalf."

"Eh? I'm not?"

"You're a temporary employee!"

My bad, said Miguel's expression as he forced a smile.

I felt my cheeks twitching as I watched on, and I couldn't help but notice that the light in Marion's eyes was very nearly snuffed out. Halphys and Garkie were similarly speechless, taken aback by this scene.

"Actually, my retired grandfather was appointed acting director of the Ministry of the Arcane, so he picked me to help him out. Lang kicked me to the curb and ordered me to come here..."

"Didn't *you* offer to bring everything?" Marion pointed out.

Miguel's forced smile was starting to get on my nerves. Yep—I could tell what this guy was like from a mile away, although I didn't want to.

He was *that* kind of person. I hated to admit it, but he and I were birds of a feather. He was just more self-conscious than I was, and not as nice.

"Can you please stop with that unsavory charade?" Marion asked. "It gets on my nerves."

"Oh, you'll forgive me for being so obnoxious? I'm not really cut out for all this formal brownnosing. No matter what I do, people always think I'm disreputable anyway, so I end up cutting corners!" Miguel chuckled, his attitude suddenly shifting.

With that, the light in Marion's eyes was finally gone. I sympathized with him, really...

"If you don't care for the formalities, let's get right down to business. Princess Anisphia, these are the documents that you requested from Lang. If there is anything else you need, please let us know. However, if you take out too many items, they will be difficult to manage. Lang told me to set a limit on how many items you can borrow from the archives at any one time."

"Understood. I'll contact you through Euphie."

"Marion and I will take care of bringing you anything you need, so don't worry!"

"Just Marion will be fine," I said, dispatching the jokester Miguel.

"Y-you don't need me?!"

I then moved on with the necessary procedures to complete the loan. After that, we were able to receive the items without further incident.

"We'll be back when you want to return them," Marion said.

"Yes. Sorry to trouble you."

"It's us at the ministry who have caused you trouble, so we should be the ones to apologize," he added with a frown.

Miguel patted him on the shoulder, and his joking attitude of a moment ago was nowhere to be seen. "We'd be really grateful for your cooperation, Princess Anisphia," he said. "He'll probably think I'm sticking my nose where it doesn't belong by saying this, but don't think too badly of Lang."

"...Why would you speak out on his behalf?"

"He's a straightforward and clumsy man. Pretty highly strung, too, and he never cuts corners. I'd like to tell him to relax for once in his life. But he's really not all that bad. He's been working behind the scenes to keep the ministry and Your Highness from getting in each other's way too much."

"Really?"

"You bet. It was his recommendation that led Princess Euphyllia to Marion in the first place, right? Right, Marion?" he said, glancing to his companion for confirmation.

Marion nodded. "I was recommended both because I'm close to her in age and because I belong to the neutral faction, so I can act as an intermediary between the more polarized ones."

"I didn't realize that..."

"He's serious and down to earth. I know you don't have a positive impression of him, but he has his own reasons for doing what he does, so please give him the benefit of the doubt."

"I have no intention of getting into any arguments with the ministry. But if they come at me with false accusations, I *will* respond accordingly."

"I'm glad to hear that. I hope we can keep being friends in the future."

"Not with you."

"Wh-whaaat?!"

"Oh, come on now!" Marion cried out. "Let's go back already, Miguel! We still have more work to do!" Having reached the end of his patience, he bowed to us with an unreadable expression and all but dragged Miguel away.

"D-do your best, Marion…," Halphys said.

"Good luck, Marion…," Garkie added.

Still being dragged off, Miguel waved back to us with that stupid smile still plastered over his face.

With the exhaustion of meeting a new acquaintance hanging over our shoulders, the three of us heaved a deep, mutual sigh.

* * *

We perused the materials borrowed from the Ministry of the Arcane in silence.

Every now and then, Garkie would groan as he closed one book and opened another. From the looks of it, he had never been particularly studious.

Halphys, on the other hand, was reading diligently, jotting down notes on a separate piece of paper when necessary. Such a dependable person—she was practically speed-reading.

They were both giving this task everything they had, so I should do the same—but instead, I was frowning more and more. I had been wondering something for a while, but here and now, that question was beginning to take shape.

"…Hey, Halphys?" I asked.

"Yes? What is it, Your Highness?"

"Maybe I'm overthinking this…but aren't our books in the Kingdom of Palettia a little hard to read?"

"Hard to…read?" Halphys put down her volume and cocked her head.

Garkie, having already taken a few short breaks, likewise glanced across at me. "In what way…?"

"Well, for instance, these documents are all records of recent events and the tax rates in each territory, right?"

"Indeed."

"And the text in them… The language is kind of…well…esoteric."

"…Esoteric?" Halphys repeated.

"A bit poetic maybe...? Or aristocratic, I guess you could say?"

"Ah...I think I see what you mean..." Garkie nodded, his gaze distant. Halphys, by contrast, looked at me askance. "Is that so...?"

"Uh-huh. That's it. Just a bit hard to follow, is all."

"But if you can't read them, you can't read any books, no?"

"No, you can't..."

That was what I meant. As far as I could tell, pretty much any book produced in the Kingdom of Palettia was filled to bursting with all these poetic phrases.

In order to understand them correctly, you needed to be educated. Meaning that if you weren't educated, you couldn't read.

From where I was standing, that seemed like a huge waste of time. When you got down to it, wasn't it strange how documents that needed to be recorded accurately were worded in such a difficult manner?

"Halphys, if you want to say it was a sunny day, is it really necessary to write about how beautiful the sky was, what scents were carried on the wind, or to speculate on what the clouds might represent?"

"...Well, it might not be necessary per se, but surely it must be useful to include details of the situation?"

"But I get the impression that books and other documents in the kingdom use all these poetic expressions that are just taken for granted. The common people communicate in much simpler sentences."

"Isn't that because most commoners can't read? It's really just well-to-do merchants and the like who interact with the nobility."

"In that sense, you could say that the common people are uneducated, and that would be the end of the conversation... I'm not saying these complicated poetic expressions are bad, but that they make it difficult to understand what the author is trying to say without specialist knowledge in *how* to read them. Don't you think?"

"...But isn't that what books are like?" Halphys asked, head cocked to one side.

True, she was probably right.

In the Kingdom of Palettia, books imparted the proper knowledge only when read by someone who had themselves received a proper education.

For that reason, claiming that books were difficult to read was essentially admitting to a lack of effort. Nonetheless, something about this whole equation left me feeling vaguely uncomfortable.

"Anis, are you still working in there?"

While I was still trying to find words for that feeling, Euphie knocked on the door and poked her head in, with Lainie standing just behind her.

"Euphie? And Lainie, too? Are you back already?"

"Hello, Princess Euphyllia, Miss Lainie." Halphys bowed politely.

"Thank you for your service!" Garkie added, following suit.

Euphie nodded to them both before turning her attention to the books laid out on the workbench.

"Are you making any progress?" she asked.

"Ah, er, well, I guess?" I answered.

"...Is something wrong?" she pressed, so I began explaining the conversation I'd just been having with Halphys.

Euphie listened on thoughtfully, chin cupped in one hand.

Lainie nodded in understanding. "It *is* difficult to understand sometimes, isn't it? I have a hard time of it, too."

"Now that you mention it, you were born a commoner, weren't you...?" Halphys asked.

"Not a commoner. I was an orphan. Even trying as hard as I could, the best I could do was memorize the letters. I had to study so hard to get into the Aristocratic Academy...," Lainie murmured, looking off into the distance.

For her part, Halphys wore a strange expression.

All of a sudden, Euphie looked up. "I understand what you're trying to say, Anis. Or your discomfort, perhaps. Maybe I can hazard a guess as to the cause."

"What's your hypothesis?"

"Essentially, the reason why documents here in the Kingdom of

Palettia are filled with all these lyrical phrases is because the nobility is comprised of mages."

"...It is?"

Why would documents need to be filled with flowery language just because they were written by mages? I waited for her to continue, unable to see the connection.

"Proficient mages can skip this, but chanting invocations is one of the first steps of using magic. And when praying to spirits, the offering is incredibly important—specifically, the amount of detail in the mental image."

"Yeah... But why are we talking about magic now?"

"I suppose the nobility has always had quite the imagination, or perhaps a habit of saying even simple things in a verbose manner. You're right, of course, Anis. Adding excessive embellishment just to convey a simple fact can make passages difficult to decipher. But the nobility takes that difficulty for granted. We have to always be aware of magic, be forever imaginative, constantly exercising our vocabulary, so we can invoke magic in more detail. So my hypothesis is that all this wordiness developed to handle magic."

"...Oh? I think I can see what you're saying. If I wanted to make a fireball, I would just say *fireball*, and that would be it. But if you're a noble, you would need to add more information, such as why it needs to be a certain size and shape, and what you're using it for. So adding more and more information is the basis of developing one's control over magic. In that case, I guess written documents *would* end up following the same pattern, then?" I asked, seeking confirmation.

"That's right." Euphie nodded. "On top of that, the books kept at the archives at the Ministry of the Arcane aren't usually read by anyone other than nobles. It's taken for granted that nobles can read them, and they don't question any of the difficult-to-understand phrasings. After all, if you know how to read them, they don't need to be written in simple sentences."

"Hmm...I suppose that makes sense... But when you're trying to research something and want to know what specifically happened, don't all these flowery and poetic phrases make it difficult to decipher the author's meaning? It's exhausting, too… It seems to me like a complete waste of time…"

With that, I could finally verbalize my thoughts. If it was readable, that was good enough. And if this was part of the Kingdom of Palettia's culture, then that was fine, too.

However, it did mean that you needed specialist knowledge if you wanted to do research or analyze statistics. At such times, all those extra collocations seemed like nothing more than extra noise.

"Um, I think there's literary value here, but for resources and reference material, the style makes them more difficult to understand," I noted.

"When you put it that way, I can see your point. I've never really noticed it before…," Euphie said.

"No, I get what Lady Anis is saying," Garkie added. "You're reading to get information, but you need to know all these special phrases ahead of time."

"It's true that they aren't really necessary, and that you would prefer that people just write the answers, but even so…" Euphie paused there with a troubled frown.

Garkie and Lainie were both nodding along in agreement with my observation. If anything, this group of ours wasn't very bookish.

The only one of us who remained quiet was Halphys, holding her hand near her mouth in silence as though pondering something.

"It would be nice to have a list of information, so you could find what you wanted at a glance…," I murmured.

"That would be difficult, I think… The Ministry of the Arcane is very busy, and it takes a lot of work to make new materials. It certainly would be useful to have a list, but if it turned into a fresh dispute…"

"You mean getting the numbers right?"

Documents in the Kingdom of Palettia were handwritten, which meant that it would take considerable labor to produce new ones. For that reason, the thought of preparing written materials before a presentation or research demonstration tended to drop me into a melancholic abyss.

Whenever I tried reforming something, it was always difficult because the essentials were lacking. Even if I wanted to procure all the necessary materials, I had to first persuade those in positions of authority to grant them to me. And then it took more materials just to bring those higher-ups around. Getting my hands on everything all took so much time and effort.

I'd be able to make much more progress if I had one of those computers from my past life... Hold on. A computer?

At that moment, a flash of inspiration coursed through my brain like an electric current.

Even if the difficulties involved in perusing these documents could be improved, it would take immeasurable effort to do so. One of those reasons was that, in this world, everything was written by hand.

But computers had been widely used in my previous life, greatly reducing the amount of time and effort required. Yet re-creating a computer would be a near impossible task, even with the help of magic.

Still, what if we were to focus just on the task of creating documents rather than everything a computer could do? There must have been tools like word processors or even typewriters in my old world, if you went back far enough in time.

What if we could mechanize such a thing, or even make a new magical tool? I picked up a pen and started jotting down the necessary functions.

I wanted to be able to input text instead of writing it all out by hand—something that would require a function to write text on paper as though stamping a seal. An input device—like a keyboard—might be nice, with buttons for each character, perhaps? And then you would need a mechanism to operate it all...

"...Anis?"

"That's it! This will work! We're going to see Tomas tomorrow!"

"...Um, Princess Anisphia?" Halphys asked.

"Ah, what are you—?" Gark started.

"She must have been struck with inspiration," Euphie remarked. "Good luck, you two."

"Eh?"

"What?"

For a moment, I could almost hear voices replete with surprise and exasperation—but I was probably just imagining things! All right—now I had to write down as many ideas as I could summon to mind!

* * *

"You want to make a magical tool that prints letters on paper...?"

"That's it!"

"...Why do I get the feeling you're up to something strange again...?"

The next day, I stormed into Tomas's workshop with Halphys and Garkie by my side.

Incidentally, after unveiling our Airdra and the special dresses for Euphie and me, we offered the craftsmen involved in constructing them all a generous reward, and a small banquet, too.

Those magical tools were still officially under development, but the government had taken a wait-and-see approach before deciding whether to introduce them more widely. For that reason, they weren't yet being mass-produced.

That being said, the ban on large-scale production could be lifted at any moment, and the craftsmen, too, were looking forward to the day when they could get hard to work making more.

Among them, Tomas was back to his regular line of work, much the same as usual.

Originally, he was an independent blacksmith. While he was receiving more requests and orders than he had before, he had returned to his previous lifestyle without joining a larger workshop, and he accepted only those projects that struck his fancy.

Seeing as he had finally managed to find a little peace, he might think I was bringing him more trouble. But I didn't care! As far as I was concerned, he was still under my employment!

"Here, this is a rough sketch of what I'm trying to do..."

He took a reluctant peek at the paper that I spread out on the workbench, while Halphys and Garkie both looked on curiously.

"Writing by hand can be tiring, so I want to make a mechanism where the letters on the board here are stamped on the paper when you press the buttons down here."

"This is more sophisticated than I thought… So you have a dial with all the letters, and it moves and prints them on the paper?"

"How about it? Do you think you can make it?"

"What kind of question is that? Looking at the shape, wouldn't you be better asking a craftsman who specializes in musical instruments?"

"Musical…? I suppose it *is* similar to a keyboard instrument."

"And that's just the input mechanism. But even if you can stamp the letters on the paper, if you want to make a full sentence, you'll have to shift this part horizontally, and you'll need some way to move to the next line. Is that even possible? If it was driven by the input device—a magical tool keyboard—it probably would be easier than writing by hand…"

"Yes! That's it! I'm trying to revolutionize document production!"

If I could do that, I would have so much more time to spare. Which would, in turn, mean that I could get around to all that other work!

"Then I'll introduce you to an instrument craftsman I know. Let's go to his workshop first."

"All right! Let's go!"

"…All right, then. Looks like I'm going to be busy again, huh?"

Tomas spoke like this was all a huge hassle, but he couldn't hide his excitement from me!

* * *

Tomas guided me to the instrument makers' workshop, where we received a generous welcome.

It seemed that word of me had spread among the craftsmen, and they were enthusiastic with their greetings, telling me that they would never have expected me to pay a visit in person.

"So the idea is to make it print letters on paper instead of producing sounds?"

"Is that possible?"

"I think we can build the letter-typing mechanism. The part we'll need to work out is how to make whole sentences rather than just single letters. But that shouldn't be too difficult."

"We ought to be able to use spirit stones to power the typing mechanism. We might be able to adapt the same process used in the Mana Blades..."

"You mean channeling magical energy into the keyboard? That's an interesting idea! I wonder if that could be applied to musical instruments as well?"

Absorbing my ideas as if they were water, the workshop manager and his artisans set about completing the blueprints.

...How should I put this? The conversation proceeded at a miraculous pace. We got a good running start, and we had a prototype ready just one week later. Even I was taken aback by the speedy development.

"Why do I feel like I'm feeding a starving beast here...?"

"They *have* been starved for development ideas, as it happens... The demonstration of the Airdra had a huge impact," Tomas told me on the way to inspecting the prototype.

Halphys was just as shocked as I was, while Garkie was struck with admiration.

The prototype unveiled at the musical instrument workshop was indeed shaped very much like a typewriter. It consisted of a dial for printing letters and a connected input device. All that remained was to place a piece of paper inside the base and start typing.

"Thank you for coming, Princess Anisphia! Please, go ahead, try it!"

"You really did finish it in just one week... In that case, allow me..."

After the workshop manager explained to me how to use it, he suggested that I take it for a test run. The keyboard seemed to be made from a composite material incorporating spirit stones, and when you passed magical energy through it, the corresponding letters were typed on the paper.

As such, there was no need to actually press the keys themselves—it was enough to simply brush your fingers against them. The characters were printed onto the paper with every touch, and with each letter, the column shifted, so line breaks posed no problems.

It was more than sufficient for a prototype. As far as I was concerned, in its current form, it was useful enough to be adopted immediately.

"This is great! Hey, Halphys, Garkie! Come and give it a try!"

"Y-yes! If you'll allow me…"

Halphys was a little hesitant at first, but once she got the hang of it, she started typing as smoothly as if she were playing the piano. The mechanism printed whole words and sentences on the white sheet of paper at a dizzying pace.

"Princess Anisphia! This is amazing! It will make writing so much easier than doing it by hand!"

"Oooh, this is good. Lots of knights out on the frontier can't write neatly, so if you let them use this, their reports will be that much easier to read."

"Ah, I think the merchants' eyes are going to sparkle when they see these."

Everyone was excitedly thinking about new ways that the prototype could be used, both by nobles and the common people alike.

Perhaps a cheaper version could also be adapted into a toy for learning letters? That would certainly help to increase literacy rates.

"This is convenient enough by itself… But if we could copy the pages, it would make bookbinding a whole lot easier, too…," I murmured under my breath.

"Copy…? Do you mean duplicating the same text?" Halphys whispered, placing a finger by her mouth.

"You could always type it out again. But even if this does simplify the process, it would still be a hassle to keep writing the same thing over and over. So I just thought it might be nice if we could make multiple copies."

"…Then couldn't you use a mechanism like in a music box?"

The moment that Halphys said this, everyone stopped moving, their mouths hanging agape. With all eyes focused on her, she raised her hands in front of her face, shaking her head frantically.

"Er, ah, um, well... It was just an idea...!"

"You said like a music box, young lady? Meaning...something that records the letters typed into it and repeats them back?"

"Y-yes. A music box plays the same tune several times over, right? So if you record the letters you type in once and automatically repeat them back, wouldn't it be possible to make multiple copies?"

"The keyboard responds to magical power, right? If we use another mechanism to record the order of the inputs, maybe it *could* be done?"

"Maybe something that marks the keys in the order they're typed so magical power could then be passed through them?"

"Can we do that?"

"Now *this* sounds interesting! Let's give it a try!"

"If it works, we might even be able to make a magical music box! It's a damn good challenge!"

"Let's do this, folks!"

"*Yeeeaaah!*" the craftsmen cried with enthusiasm in response to their leader's order.

Halphys was getting flustered from all the excitement; Garkie wore a radiant grin.

Tomas, the only one among us calmly observing the situation, let out a quiet sigh. "I *knew* this was going to turn into something big."

* * *

"And, er...so that's how we made it. And the finished product is called a Thought Board."

I wasted no time before unveiling my latest magical tool, which I had decided to call a Thought Board as the user translated their thoughts with the printing dial.

The guests invited to this demonstration were my father, my mother, and Duke Grantz, the venue being my father's office. Thank you, Garkie, for bringing it all this way! After incorporating Halphys's recording and playback functions, the device became somewhat larger than the initial prototype.

"I devised the original idea for the input mechanism, and the device itself was put together by the craftsmen in the castle town. Halphys here came up with the idea for the recording and playback functions for making duplicate copies. This single device should greatly reduce the amount of work and manpower necessary to prepare documents."

"I see…," Duke Grantz muttered as he activated the Thought Board and tried inputting text.

Because of several iterations and improvements, the device was capable not only of typing text, but also of drawing lines, which should greatly reduce the amount of effort required to create documents.

At first, the duke typed one letter at a time so as not to make any mistakes, so silent that I could see Halphys literally holding her breath.

"…Hmm…," he murmured out of the blue.

With that, he sat back in his seat with the Thought Board positioned in front of him and began operating it with both hands. It wasn't long before things started to get strange. His typing speed was quickly picking up pace.

Huh? Just as I stopped to wonder what was going on, he was typing at a truly terrifying speed—so fast that the machine risked breaking down. His fingers wriggled and slid across the keyboard as if they had minds of their own.

In the blink of an eye, fresh documents came into being—the speed calling to mind something called a *photocopier* from my past life. What on earth *was* this? It was just too fast!

"…Ha! Ha-ha-ha!"

And then, laughter. Whose laughter? I could hardly believe my ears, but it was coming from Duke Grantz.

A small yelp escaped Halphys's lips. Garkie had broken out into a cold sweat, his face twitching uncomfortably.

Duke Grantz, directly in my line of sight, was smiling so devilishly that even monsters would flee at the sight.

Every now and then, another chuckle would escape his lips, as if at some fond memory. All the while, the Thought Board continued to print letters with frightening momentum—one document after another. And he wasn't just typing random keys.

"…This is a wonderful thing you've created, Princess Anisphia!"

Why did that joyous voice fill me with cold dread? All I could do was force a friendly smile.

At Duke Grantz's request, we relinquished the demonstration Thought Board to his custody.

He was moving so fast I could hardly see him! I couldn't see anything but Duke Grantz typing an endless stream of documents with that evil grin on his face.

But just as I was about to avert my eyes from this unbelievable reality, my father spoke out in a gentle voice: "Anis."

"I can't see anything."

"No, look carefully. Observe how excited he is. If he can keep up that momentum, I can foresee a future where we'll have much more work to do. Wouldn't you agree?"

"I-is that a *good* thing…?"

"Indeed it is, Anis. Would you be able to produce more of them on short notice?" he asked.

"You wouldn't demonstrate it if you couldn't mass-produce them, would you?" my mother added.

They were both grinning, but those grins didn't reach their eyes at all. They grabbed me by the shoulders with such force that I feared they might break my arms.

I looked to Halphys and Garkie for help, but both averted their gazes without a moment's delay. *Don't abandon me here, you two!*

"My dear, loyal daughter…you wouldn't let Grantz run unchecked and ruin *my* job, would you?"

"Yes, you're too kind. Can you do it, Anis?"

My father and mother approached from either side, both of them whispering under their breath. There was something very unusual about the firmness with which they were gripping my shoulders.

In the meantime, Duke Grantz was still happily playing away with the Thought Board. He could afford to pay a little more attention to us here, couldn't he? *Hey, are you listening, Duke Grantz?!*

"But if this becomes widespread, magical tools will render other forms of bookmaking obsolete..."

"Hmm...I don't think handwritten manuscripts will go out of style anytime soon, even if people do learn about this."

All of a sudden, my parents grew very quiet, only whispering to each other with troubled expressions. Come to think of it, a revolution in bookmaking *would* change the way people worked...

"If the ability to read was a given, couldn't people be hired as assistants to public officials or the like?"

"Assistants to public officials...?"

"There would have to be jobs for record keepers, or to check for misspellings in letters..."

"Orphans, do you think we could honestly find enough people to perform all those checks if Grantz is capable of working at this rate?"

"Impossible. If the ability to read can be taken as a given for our people, then a period of education might make them into productive members of society. This could have a huge impact on book production in the future, so this might be a good chance to increase the workforce."

"In that case, let's adopt this idea of Anis's."

"Hmm. Let's propose it at our next meeting, along with this Thought Board. Never mind the craftspeople—there are many noble children sulking because they missed the opportunity to become bureaucrats," my father said.

"We're counting on you, Anis," my mother added.

"Y-yes...," I stammered, doing my best to respond to my parents with a smile.

When finally I was freed from that pressure, I ran to the castle town as fast as I could and bowed my head. The craftsmen cried out with cheers of accomplishment and joy at the huge order to produce more devices. Only then did the light in my eyes fade.

Thus, thanks to the passionate promotion of my father and those in the palace, the Thought Board took off in popularity at astonishing speed—and at the same time, the screams of new recruits hired as assistant bureaucrats began to echo throughout the palace.

I—I didn't do anything wrong!

CHAPTER 4
Signs of Change

A month had passed since the inadvertent explosive introduction of my Thought Board, an incident that had come to be known as "Duke Magenta's fit of madness."

During this time, Thought Boards had appeared throughout the royal palace, met with both joy and lamentation—the former for the reduction of manual labor and the latter by those who now had more work on their hands because of streamlined operations.

Maybe it was just my imagination that the new administrative assistants seemed lost in grief. *Duke Grantz, it isn't a toy, you know? Are you really just working? I see...*

Incidentally, I had also heard from Euphie that the Thought Board had proven to be of great benefit at the Ministry of the Arcane, and the various factions were beginning to coalesce around her.

No matter how complicated their feelings were when it came to me, the fact was that these Thought Boards could streamline paperwork to such an extent that people couldn't keep their hands off them. Nonetheless, they were still reluctant to ask me for more units directly, terrified that I would refuse to turn them over to the ministry.

As such, to my relief, Euphie took up the mantle of dealing with negotiations. As far as I was concerned, if work at the ministry could be made more efficient, the documents there would be better organized, so I had no complaints.

My work in recent weeks consisted mainly of product checks and deliveries, and of building up a support base when I greeted customers.

Incidentally, my father asked me to wait at least two months before coming out with any more magical tools. I was fully aware that I had caused a huge commotion this time around. *I'm sorry. I'll try not to do it again.*

The task of confirming deliveries left us with a good amount of spare time, so it had become our routine to spend those hours gathering information from books borrowed from the Ministry of the Arcane and setting them out in new documents.

Halphys was particularly adept at this kind of work and set about it with diligent efficiency. She was so dexterous, in fact, that at times I wondered whether she might not be able to handle it all on her own.

Garkie, on the other hand, was no good at it at all. He simply wasn't made for desk work and was always quick to throw in the towel.

His natural response when he couldn't get away from his desk was to sink into melancholy, so instead of keeping him at my workshop in the detached palace, we set out to inspect the Royal Guard instead.

"Ah, how's it coming? Have you all gotten used to handling Mana Blades?"

In front of me, several knights each equipped with a Mana Blade of their own stood facing each other.

A special unit of knights from the Royal Guard had been established to operate the Mana Blades that I had provided them with on a trial basis, and it was this group of warriors who now stood before us ready to exchange blows.

Among them was one knight supervising as their leader; I knew his face well. When he saw me, he broke into a broad smile.

He was a big man, his stern face somewhat intimidating when he was silent. But when he offered up a smile, his charm and kindness shone through.

"Well now, Princess Anisphia. Thank you for joining us."

"Hello, Baron Cyan."

It was Baron Dragus Cyan, Lainie's father. The baron had been elevated to the nobility after a successful career as an adventurer and now served as an instructor for the knight unit set up to test my magical tools.

As a former commoner, he was unable to use magic—but because of that, he had a quick understanding of magical tools and a wealth of other experiences to draw on, which was why he was selected for this leadership role.

I couldn't deny the nepotism at play, but thanks to the baron's background as an adventurer, I found it very easy to communicate with him. As far as I was concerned, he was the perfect person for the job.

"How is everyone handling the Mana Blades?"

"We're learning more day by day. I hope we'll be able to introduce them more broadly soon. Some of us are a little uncertain about them, given that they feel less substantial than regular swords, but they're more than effective even as backup weapons. They should help when dealing with magic-capable monsters, too," the baron answered with his undaunted ever-dependable grin.

He had been far from the front lines for many years now, but from what I gathered, he had never let up with his training. When it came to swordsmanship, he was up there with the strongest of knights.

And it wasn't only his skill with a blade that fueled his impressive reputation. He had the courage and calmness of mind to assess just about any situation and face it without fear.

No, it wasn't just martial skill that had helped him rise to the top. He may have only held the rank of baron, but he still had considerable clout and influence.

Compared to born-and-bred nobles, he wasn't without his rough edges. But all the same, I thought he was doing very well for a self-made baron.

Surprisingly, teaching swordsmanship seemed to have turned into a full-on vocation for him. From what I heard, he had been all but dedicated himself to it ever since Lainie had taken up work at the detached palace.

He'd gone through a good amount of hardship after the incident surrounding his daughter, but I was honestly happy to see that things were finally turning around.

"It's been a while, Baron Cyan."

"Thanks for your service!"

"Ah, Master Gark and Miss Halphys. I heard you've been exerting yourself under Princess Anisphia's care. I'm glad to see you're both in good health."

As my two attendants greeted him, Baron Cyan's hardened expression softened a touch.

An instructor at the Royal Guard, he must have been familiar with them both. As the three individuals exchanged relaxed greetings, he turned his gaze once more to the squad of knights wielding their Mana Blades.

"They might be getting the hang of it, but they still can't hold a candle to you, Your Highness. You really are incredible."

"...Huh? I don't think it's all that hard to wield a Mana Blade, though...?"

"What are you saying? You can freely adjust the length and reach of your blade, no? That skill isn't easy to master."

"It's just a matter of adjusting the amount of magic and changing the shape of the sword to reach your desired target, though, you know?" I pointed out.

"That's easy enough to say. But what do you think, Master Gark?" the baron asked. "You're one of the most proficient knights in the royal guard when it comes to using magical tools, after all."

"Isn't it pretty scary, suddenly changing the distance between you and your target? And you've got to make all these minute adjustments *while* fighting. If you can't put it together properly, you'll drag your allies into the middle of the action. And I don't know if you'd be able to parry an attack from the side before you can retract an extended blade," Garkie answered with a sullen look.

His lips were pursed into a thin line as he pondered the difficulties. Halphys, too, wore a forced smile.

Taking in their reactions, Baron Cyan let out an amused chuckle. "It seems you don't have a very good sense of your own expertise, Princess Anisphia."

"Hmm...I guess not..."

It was certainly true that I lacked confidence in my assessments of myself lately. On the other hand, though, I felt it wouldn't be right to just accept this praise as is, so in the end, I could say nothing.

"Baron Cyan! Do you mind if we interrupt?"

"Hmm? What is it?"

In the midst of our conversation, the knights who had been training gathered around us.

Maybe it was just time for them to take a break, I wondered—and that was when their collective gaze focused on me.

"If you could spare a moment, Princess Anisphia, could you teach us the trick to using Mana Blades?!" The enthusiasm in the knight's voice almost knocked me over.

And after the first, a barrage of additional requests just kept on coming.

"Hmm... How about it, Princess Anisphia?" the baron asked.

"I suppose I could give a demonstration. I'm afraid I can't instruct each and every person here, but maybe someone could volunteer as a sparring partner?"

"If it's all right with you, Princess Anisphia. In that case...let's ask Master Gark to be your partner."

"Eh?" Garkie turned to Baron Cyan in surprise. "Are you sure?"

"You're the most suited, I think, Master Gark. Does anyone have any objections?" Baron Cyan asked the group.

The other knights were unanimous—leaving Garkie to turn his gaze to them all in bewilderment.

"Are you really that strong, Garkie?" I asked out of an abundance of curiosity.

"No, it's not like that!" he exclaimed, shaking his head furiously.

His fellow knights were quick to suggest otherwise:

"In terms of overall ability, Gark isn't really all that exceptional. And that includes magic."

"But in single-weapon swordsmanship, there aren't many people who can break past him."

"I've only ever seen him lose to the knight commander and Baron Cyan."

"...So he really is an incredible swordsman?" I asked again, and the other knights broke into conflicted frowns.

"His attacks are fairly average...but he's really good at defense."

"Unless you use magic to break past his guard, you won't have any chance of winning."

"So when it comes to drawing out the full strength of his opponent, Gark comes first in the whole Royal Guard!"

"...I suppose that does pique my interest," I said. "Garkie, shall we go a round?"

"...If you order me to, I'll have no choice but to obey," he answered with a resigned shrug, although it wasn't long before he was swinging his arms in circles.

After receiving the Celestial, it had been a long time since I had last used a regular Mana Blade. I accepted two units while Garkie armed himself just with the one as we positioned ourselves across from each other.

The knights were standing in a line by one side, with Baron Cyan in the center as referee and Halphys waiting nearby.

"In that case, let's see what you can do. I, Dragus Cyan, shall stand witness. Both of you, bow to your opponent!"

As was customary, Garkie and I each offered the other a bow before assuming our fighting stances. Garkie kept a low center of gravity, holding his sword out slightly less than horizontal. His eyes, open just a fraction, were fully alert, on the lookout for any sudden movements.

My first attack, aimed at his neck, was intended simply to sound him out—and he met it with a leaping strike.

From there, we launched into an exchange of sword blows. When the Mana Blade in my right hand was repelled, I lashed out next with the one in my left. This back-and-forth between offense and defense cycled several times through, with Garkie parrying everything from downward strikes to diagonal slashes and the occasional thrust.

"…Ha-ha…" Weak laughter escaped my throat.

I had been attacking nonstop for a while now, but not once had Garkie attempted to fight back. It was true that I hadn't exactly given him any openings to counter, but I couldn't stop myself from chuckling.

Besides, he hadn't moved so much as a single step.

Of course, he turned his body to meet my blows—but that was all. It was as though he was stepping only within a clearly defined circle.

But even so, I couldn't land a single strike. His sword as he parried was too fast, too adroit.

He reacted almost immediately to my attacks. His own strikes as he parried were minimal, and he wasted no time before returning to his defensive stance.

No matter what angle I lashed out from or what fighting techniques I adopted, I couldn't break his guard. A sense of apprehension was building up inside me. Launching into a reckless wide swing in an attempt to end this impasse would risk leaving myself hopelessly open.

I felt as if I were swinging my swords against a brick wall. His own blade was huge, unwavering, and yet incredibly adept.

Every time our weapons crossed, I could see it—this was the product of arduous study and refinement. Garkie aimed for the top with a fool's tenacity, as though publicly declaring that he would overcome any blow.

There was no dance-like beauty, flair, or spectacle about it. His was a technique honed for maximum precision with minimal movement. His sword forms were unassuming and austere—yet that only lent them a different kind of beauty.

And that wasn't all—I was shaken by the sheer force and power of his spirit as he threw every ounce of effort into this task. There weren't many opponents who could send a physical chill coursing down my spine during a duel. If I had to pick anyone close, it would be Euphie.

But this is crazy; I can't even break him down anywhere close to her.

It might have been true that Garkie wasn't particularly skilled at offense. Maybe he was overly cautious, as he didn't seek to take advantage of the openings that I intentionally left for him.

If I had been fighting Euphie, I would've been so afraid that she would use her powerful magic to turn the situation around that I would have fought as hard as I could, hoping to rapidly break through her defenses.

But put another way, Garkie wasn't equipped to turn the tables on me in quite the same way—and as such, I had time to concentrate on my attacks.

Yet I still couldn't land a blow. No matter what I did, he met my every move with a skillful parry. His swordsmanship was built on a strong foundation, so he could respond immediately to any moves.

This was much easier said than done, yet Garkie had pulled it off. I doubted that even he realized just how amazing that was.

I wouldn't be able to win this bout through swordsmanship alone. I might not lose, but I wouldn't win, either. I could see why the other knights had spoken so peculiarly about him.

"…You're incredible, Garkie," I said, trying to catch my breath. "You've really put a lot of effort into mastering all this, haven't you? You're so much stronger than when we first met."

"I'm honored by your praise," he responded calmly.

He didn't seem tired at all, nor did he come across as agitated or upset. He was so stolid that I almost wondered whether he wasn't actually a golem or something.

In terms of physical size and strength, Garkie came out on top. I had been neglecting my training recently, so I was almost out of breath. I would have to redouble my efforts, I told myself, my lips curling into a grin.

"…Garkie, do you mind if I give myself a physical power boost?"

"That's fine."

"Thanks. Then here I go!"

I concentrated my attention on the Impressed Seal on my back and drew on my dragon magic. Then, directing that outflow of power into my legs, I dashed right for Garkie.

For the first time, Garkie actively adjusted his position, backing away to lessen the force of the impact as he received the blow.

"Gah…!"

His expression, until now stolid and unmoved, distorted with pain. I suspected that he, too, was using a physical enhancement, but mine definitely had the greater power.

So in terms of raw strength, I should have been by far superior—and yet I still couldn't break past his walls.

He had a way of fighting that was completely different from mine, which I had cultivated through my own intuitions and combat experience—his sword technique was more stubbornly honest and direct.

I was quite sure that we had both focused our efforts in the same direction. He must have mastered this because he hadn't taken shortcuts like I had.

If this duel could be decided by one's skill with a blade alone, Garkie would have been the one more worthy of victory. Which was precisely why I thought this was such a horrible waste.

For instance, if only he had a teacher who could guide him to yet greater heights.

Or if only he had a rival with whom he could compete toe-to-toe.

Because Garkie's sword was focused entirely on itself, it seemed to be missing something.

"You're skilled, really. But…!"

I leaped backward and swung my Mana Blades in an arc. The distance between the two of us continued to grow, but one of the weapons, extending in length as I fell back, was still aimed for Garkie's flank.

Bracing himself firmly against the ground, he moved to catch that attack with a decisive parry.

At that moment, I deactivated the first Mana Blade and poured my energy into the second one, boosting its output.

I did this only after I was sure that Garkie would attempt to catch the blow, giving myself an opening to catch up to his reaction time. Then, in order to finally get around his defenses, I amplified the output of my Mana Blade, spinning around and leaping forward.

I strengthened my body and closed the gap in an instant, maximizing the power output of my weapon. Garkie, having moved to block my previous blow, stiffened for a moment, but his body reacted without delay.

Our Mana Blades collided, letting out a flood of sparks—and the magical edge began to flex.

It changed form like a whip, its tip shooting for Garkie's neck. Just before it could make contact, he froze in place.

With a pitiful expression washing over his face, he let out a deep, disbelieving sigh.

"...I concede," he declared, hanging his head.

At that moment, the knights surrounding us let out a tremendous, wild cheer, leaving Baron Cyan to try to calm them down.

"Thank you, both of you," the baron said. "I'm sure that will prove to have been a valuable lesson for future study. You were excellent, Princess Anisphia. And Master Gark, your skill was a sight to behold as well."

"When it comes to Mana Blades, I'm not willing to give up," I said. "But if it was normal swordsmanship, Garkie would have had me beat."

"Not at all. I had my hands full with defense... And you're so fast, Lady Anis. Even if I manage to keep up with one move, I can't catch the next one in time. You're brilliant," Garkie said with a refreshing smile.

He didn't seem to regret having lost at all. If anything, *I* was the one who felt contrite.

I had been slacking off lately and was getting a bit sluggish. I would have to put a little more time in to focus on my training.

* * *

After my training bout with Garkie, we left the other knights and joined Baron Cyan in a separate room. The endless praise and questioning didn't stop until we were firmly away.

Shortly after we'd entered, a maid arrived to lay out tea, and after we had finished quenching our thirst, Baron Cyan offered up his own words of appreciation: "I know that was a sudden request, so thank you for going along with it. Watching you two duel will spur the rest of them to double down."

"If it helps popularize magical tools, I don't mind," I replied. "If there's anything else I can do to help, please let me know, Baron Cyan."

"Thank you for your encouraging words. Ever since I was given this role, my days have been very fulfilling indeed," he said with a gentle smile.

I first met Baron Cyan during Lainie's audience with my father following the incident with my brother's engagement. Given how pale he had turned during that encounter, he seemed very happy to be able to spend his time like this now.

But while I was reflecting on all this, something about his mood changed. He looked as though he wanted to broach another subject but was conflicted and unable to speak up.

"Baron Cyan? Did you ask me to come here so that you could talk to me about something?"

"...I'm sorry. I must have let it show. This is rather embarrassing."

"I don't mind... What's troubling you?"

"It's not about business... It's about family. But I can't say that you're completely uninvolved, Your Highness, so I've been debating with myself whether I should bring it up."

"Family? Has something happened...?"

"Given that reaction, I suppose Lainie hasn't said anything. In that case, I suppose it wouldn't be out of line for me to tell you..."

"Ah... That would be like her, keeping quiet."

Lainie was a modest young woman with a strong sense of responsibility, so it was only natural that she wouldn't want to trouble others with family affairs.

But all the same, how exactly could this issue within the Cyan family concern *me*? I couldn't begin to guess.

"You can tell Lainie I forced it from you, so will you share it with me?"

"...Um, Your Highness? Perhaps Gark and I should leave?" Halphys asked, glancing nervously back and forth between the baron and me.

I looked at Baron Cyan to confirm, but he shook his head. "I don't mind. I would be grateful, actually, if you would listen. There's a possibility you may suffer the same calamity."

"Calamity...?"

"...My family is currently being inundated with marriage proposals for Lainie."

"Huh? Marriage proposals?"

My eyebrows rose at this unexpected turn. Halphys and Garkie likewise appeared stunned.

Baron Cyan, having confided in me, looked visibly distressed. "As I'm sure you know, Lainie has been going to the Ministry of the Arcane as Princess Euphyllia's secretary, and she seems to have attracted a fair amount of attention... I would say perhaps thirty percent of the proposals are serious, and the other seventy percent the result of careful calculation."

"Ah...I see. The possibility of that completely slipped my mind," I groaned, placing a hand against my forehead.

I *had* heard from Euphie that Lainie seemed to be quite popular of late.

Lainie had always been polite, earnest, and affable. Plus, she was extremely skilled at using her vampire abilities to get close to people's hearts. They were almost unfairly powerful, and combined with her charming personality, they gave her a natural advantage.

Apparently, her presence had also helped to soothe ties at the Ministry of the Arcane. Even those who might otherwise have wanted to move closer to Euphie but were reluctant to do so owing to their status or position were now speaking out thanks to Lainie's mediation and recommendation.

Behind the scenes, her vampiric mental interference abilities were exerting their effect. She wasn't directly trying to influence them—only to glean what she could about their emotions. Her responses to those emotions were kind and sincere, so people tended to relax around her and react favorably.

Of course, those who were hostile or had malevolent plans would keep their distance. I'd heard that such individuals had attempted to interfere on several occasions, but Euphie had responded resolutely to each of them.

As a result, things were apparently proceeding well. But hearing Baron Cyan open up to me, I began to wonder whether Lainie might not have been exerting *too* strong an effect.

"Unlike Euphie and I, Lainie is the daughter of a baron, a noble who rose from the rank of commoner. Anyone who wants to get close to us might see her as a valuable prize…"

"If the suitor is from a baron family like me, or a viscount like my wife's family, then we can refuse," Baron Cyan said. "But when it comes to counts and marquises…"

"Have there been any offers from them?"

"Yes… Many."

"I suppose that makes sense. There are a lot of high-ranking nobles at the Ministry of the Arcane…"

It would indeed be difficult for Baron Cyan to deal with all that—nigh impossible, really. It would only cause trouble in the future to refuse a proposal from a high-ranking noble family.

"Lainie says she wants to work as a maid-in-waiting, and that she has no intention of getting married in the future," he told me. "So we have to decline these offers, but we can't afford to provoke a dispute with any high-ranking nobles. So while it pains me to do this, my only choice is to ask for your help, Your Highness."

"Yes, I think that's the best response," I agreed.

Indeed, if Baron Cyan couldn't directly turn down the offers given his family's lower rank, it was only natural that he would turn to us. Actually, that would be in our interests, too…

"The thing is, Lainie seems to be having a hard time dealing with it all," he continued. "She asked me to keep this from Your Highness and Princess Euphyllia for now, saying she would tell you both herself…"

"If these offers were coming from interested individuals, I might agree with you there," I said. "But if they're just trying to get close to me or

Euphie, it isn't just a problem for her. I wish someone would have told me earlier, actually."

"I'm sorry…"

"I'll give Lainie a scolding later for keeping secrets."

If we started interfering with Lainie's engagement proposals, we would probably invite criticism from society at large. No doubt the reason why she hadn't brought it up herself was because she was worried about that possibility.

Lainie getting married wasn't only a problem between different factions, but also one that affected her and us.

To be perfectly honest, given that she had no choice but to conceal her vampire nature from others, it would be difficult for her to marry in the conventional way.

That was why I wanted her to rely on us more often. Perhaps she had too strong a sense of responsibility? No doubt those feelings were mixed in with guilt and trauma.

"Baron Cyan, everything you've told me…"

"I heard that Master Gark here isn't engaged, and that Miss Halphys, well… There's been a lot of talk lately, so it got me thinking about my own family."

A pall seemed to fall over Halphys at the baron's remarks. "Thank you for your concern…"

"Are you having difficulties, too, Halphys?" I asked.

"I've been asked to annul my engagement to Marion. Count Antti is now one of the most powerful nobles at the Ministry of the Arcane, so a lot of people seem to be interested in pursuing him even if he isn't the direct heir," she explained.

I rested a hand on my forehead as I let out a deep sigh.

I understood full well how important it was for noble families to build lasting bonds and how some arranged marriages purely on a contractual basis, regardless of the affections of the parties involved.

But I couldn't stand to watch that unfortunate story play out around me. Especially if it ended up causing grief.

"You can always talk to me, too, if you've got any problems, Halphys. You know that, right?"

"Thank you, Princess Anisphia. I will consult with you if circumstances exceed my control. It will probably be fine, I hope...," she told me with a troubled frown.

I could only watch on speechlessly in reply.

* * *

"It's fine to keep secrets, Lainie, but there are some things you shouldn't hide, you know?"

That night, after finishing dinner at the detached palace, I broached the topic during our usual conversation time.

Lainie stiffened, while Euphie and Ilia gave her a quizzical look.

"Um, what are you talking about, Lady Anis...?" she asked.

"I met Baron Cyan today."

"...Father..."

I could make out a soft moan as she hung her head, lifting a hand to cover her eyes.

"Did you think you could handle it all yourself? If you did, that was daft of you. You didn't tell us because you didn't want to cause any trouble, right?"

"Ugh..."

"Anis? Did something happen to Lainie?" Euphie asked.

"...You've been with her a lot lately," I answered. "Have you noticed anything out of the ordinary?"

"...Not that I can think of."

"What about the reactions of the people around her?"

"More people have opened their hearts to her, I think. The mood at the Ministry of the Arcane seems to have lifted a little, too... Ah." She paused there, placing a finger on her wrinkled brow as she released a deep exhale. "I completely forgot... Is *that* what this is?"

"...Ah. She's received a marriage proposal, I take it?" Ilia surmised, glancing back to her for confirmation.

93

Lainie averted her gaze, staring off into tomorrow as she sank into silence.

"I heard you've been approached by the sons of counts and marquises?" I asked. "It'll be impossible for your father to turn down offers like that, you realize? If he mishandles them, he'll get into all sorts of trouble."

"...I know. But..."

"If you think you can just talk to them yourself, that isn't going to work, either, right? I'm sure you know Euphie and I will help if they try to lay a hand on you, but there's still a chance things could go very wrong."

Whether they were driven into a corner or had blind faith in their own actions, there was no telling what someone chasing after her might do. But I couldn't say all that out loud—it didn't sound convincing even to me.

"You need to be more *aware*, Lainie," I continued. "I don't want anything to happen to you. Your powers are that important. And I'm worried about you, too. If you're in trouble, we'll do our best to help you. We care about you."

"That's right," Euphie added. "If not for you, we might not be gathered here like this today. And I'm saddened to hear you didn't want to lean on us for support. You offered to accompany me to the ministry because you wanted to help, didn't you?"

"That's... I wanted to return the favor...not to bother you all even more..."

"You've basically ended up treating us as strangers, Lainie. Trust goes both ways."

"I wonder whether my own lack of courage didn't put extra pressure on you. You don't have to worry about problems of this kind."

"Lady Anis... Lady Euphyllia..."

Our words brought Lainie to tears. She tried to wipe them away with her finger before anyone could notice, but the tears simply kept on coming.

"If any one of us was missing, we wouldn't have the relationships that we have today. It's not like everything that has happened up till now has been right, and we've all made mistakes, but even so...I know you don't want to cause trouble for everyone around you, but I want you to understand how important you are to all of us as well."

"...Yes."

"I'm sorry I didn't realize all this sooner," Euphie added. "I didn't figure it out on my own, and you couldn't bring it up, either. It must have been hard keeping it bottled up inside all this time, no?"

Sniffling, Lainie turned her head from side to side. Even from a slight distance, I could see her trembling as she labored for breath, no doubt fighting to hold back her sobs.

After giving her a moment to calm down, I continued, "Lainie, tell your father that you're declining the proposals because Euphie and I both want you to remain at the detached palace as our attendant. We'll respond directly to any high-ranking nobles that you can't turn down on your own, so let us know who we need to contact."

"I'm sorry... I'll tell my father..."

"That's all right," I said. "We're partly to blame here, too. We anticipated something like this, but we didn't take adequate precautions."

"That's right. Considering your position, you're an easy target. And you *are* adorable, Lainie," Euphie added.

"L-Lady Euphyllia?" Flustered, Lainie flushed bright red—prompting Euphie to burst out laughing.

Perhaps realizing that she was being teased, Lainie puffed out her cheeks and fixed Euphie with a glare.

The two of them were soon smiling at one another so warmly that I couldn't help smiling, too. Considering the circumstances of their first meeting, it was a real miracle that they now got along so well.

But when I looked away, I caught sight of Ilia watching—staring at Lainie as though her thoughts lay elsewhere.

The indescribable, almost dangerous glint in her eyes brought a frown to my face.

Hmm, this is making me kind of uneasy. I should probably come up with a strategy to deal with this soon. But then again, Lainie's feelings are important, too... What should I do?

No matter how much Euphie and I wanted to protect her, there would always be those who would come chasing after her. The course of action that I had suggested didn't solve the fundamental problem.

We could try to find someone to whom we could reveal her unique circumstances and stage a fake engagement, but something told me that Lainie herself wouldn't appreciate that.

I hoped that events wouldn't spiral out of control, but I still had my worries. I let out a weak sigh, my thoughts turning to the potential problems that might lay ahead.

CHAPTER 5
The Troubles of a Vampire Girl

I, Lainie Cyan, could probably sum up my life to date with one phrase: full of ups and downs.

I grew up on the road with my mother. I was very young at the time, and my memories from back then are few and far between.

I can't even remember her face. But I know that she was a kind and loving parent. Which is why I remember just how painful it was to say goodbye to her.

During our travels, my mother fell ill and never returned. I was placed in an orphanage, as seemed to have been arranged in advance.

What pushed me further into depression after losing my mother were the quarrels with other children from the orphanage. One boy would be mean to me, then another would grab him and start yelling. Then the girls would go around calling me conceited and impertinent.

As I grew into an adult, I came to accept such days as the reality of my everyday life—then I met a man claiming to be my father. To my surprise, he was a noble, and I was taken back to his household as a nobleman's daughter.

And now I was working as a personal lady-in-waiting to the kingdom's two princesses.

Looking back, so many things had taken place. I had been caught up in Prince Algard's conspiracy and then rescued by Lady Anis and Lady Euphyllia. I still had a strong impression of that time, so much so that I frequently relived it in my dreams.

Having learned that I was a vampire and not a regular human being, I would have been unable to object if everyone had decided to behead me on the spot as a danger to society. I truly was grateful from the very bottom of my heart to all those who had stood by me and offered their guidance. And I wanted to repay them for their generosity.

"...That's all there is to it," I murmured, the words sounding vague and forlorn even to me.

Soaking in the bathtub at the detached palace, I lost myself in thought.

My duties of late were to assist Lady Euphyllia. I delivered documents to the various departments of the ministry, listened to numerous petitions to her, and attended meetings to read the emotions of those present and gauge their degree of favorability.

This was all thanks to my vampire powers, and I conveyed everything that I learned to Lady Euphyllia so that she could build stronger relationships with those at the ministry.

And from what I could tell, it was actually working. I was so happy and proud to have been of use to her.

So to be perfectly honest, all these engagement proposals now were essentially the result of a miscalculation. I had never thought that I, the root cause of so many problems thus far, would be seen as a prospective bride.

I was the one who had misled Prince Algard, who had been next in line to become king. How could anyone want me? It was inconceivable. But if someone was trying to get close to Lady Anis or Lady Euphyllia, it did make sense. As was often the case with nobles, marriage was chiefly about forging familial connections and protecting one's rights and interests.

And so I hadn't wanted to get engaged to anyone. I didn't want to be partnered with someone who had ulterior motives, and of course, I was a vampire. If I had children, that condition would most likely be passed down to them, too.

To be perfectly frank, I was a little taken aback by it all. I felt nothing when my suitors told me they were in love, or how they felt that we were destined to be together. None of it resonated with me because I didn't believe in it in the first place.

I was utterly convinced—I wasn't suited for life as a nobleman's daughter. Some of these suitors seemed to genuinely like me, but still I found them a nuisance.

…At times, I considered myself heartless, and I hated myself for it. I just wanted to repay everyone's kindness toward me. How I wished that were the only thing on my mind.

"Lainie, are you still in there?"

"W-wah?! Mistress I-Ilia?!"

I was so taken aback by the sudden voice calling out to me that I flailed in the bathtub. Turning toward the voice, I realized that Ilia was standing nearby.

Her reddish-brown hair, which she usually wore tied up in a bun, was hanging loose over her shoulders. When she took off her clothes, her body, so beautiful that it would catch the eye regardless of one's gender, was left fully exposed. I was accustomed to seeing her in her normal state of dress, so this behavior now left me with a completely different impression of her.

"Are you still in there?"

"N-no! I'm almost finished! I'll go before I get in your way!"

"…It's no bother. Could you wait here a short while?"

"Hm?"

"I wanted to talk to you for a bit, Lainie."

Once again, I was caught on the back foot. Had I made a mistake somewhere? Had I done something to upset her? My heart was pounding for an altogether different reason now.

Saying no wasn't an option here. So I simply kept watching as she washed her body.

…She really leaves a completely different impression when she lets her hair down.

Ilia had always had a slight mischievous streak, but she was ultimately a straitlaced individual dedicated to her work. She didn't let trivial matters upset her, and she could handle just about anything on her own.

From the moment that she had started teaching me how to serve as a lady's attendant, she had been incredible. And I adored her like a teacher.

She loved me, too, or so it seemed to me. Instead of pampering or spoiling me, she would scold me harshly and do her best to set me straight. For that reason, I felt a little defensive when she suggested that she wanted to talk.

I groaned slightly, unsure what to do. The next moment, Ilia was done washing up and tied her hair back with a towel to keep it from getting wet, then she sat down next to me in the bathtub.

I was transfixed by her beauty. Perhaps this was the allure that came with physical maturity; in any event, I couldn't help feeling restless.

Though she sat immediately beside me, she didn't say anything for a little while. The silence felt heavy. So I stole a glance at her.

This was a bad idea, or so I was about to say when finally she spoke up. "Have you calmed down a little?"

"Huh? Ah… You mean about what happened at dinner? I'm all right now."

I had teared up hearing Lady Anis's and Lady Euphyllia's generous comments earlier this evening. Ilia was surely concerned for me.

I really was surrounded by wonderful people. What could this be if not a blessing? I wanted to cherish this feeling that had taken root in my heart.

As I was thinking all this, Ilia turned her gaze toward me, her eyes seemingly concealing a hidden melancholy of their own.

"…Are you really all right?" she asked.

"I am. Really."

"But it must be such a burden, no? To think you've received engagement proposals from various gentlemen. Even Lady Euphyllia has been taking precautions ever since the incident."

"That's…"

Now that Ilia had pointed it out, I was confronted with the reality of what I had only vaguely sensed might be the case.

I, too, had noticed how Lady Euphyllia had taken to maintaining a certain distance from the male sex. There were a great many male employees at the Ministry of the Arcane, some of whom seemed to have ulterior motives toward her.

Whenever she herself sensed that that might be the case, she adopted such a cold demeanor that even I felt shivers coursing down my spine.

"It's because of what happened to her engagement with Prince Algard, isn't it? She's never said so out loud, but maybe that's just out of concern for me...?"

"No doubt. She has a wounded heart. Just like you, Lainie."

"...Me?"

"You're both in very different positions, but you're hurting just as much as she is. I'm worried it might have become a burden for you."

"...I wonder? I don't know if I'd say that, though."

"If you're sure. But I still worry."

"...You do...?"

My heart warmed to hear her reaching out like this—and a creeping sensation that almost made me want to squirm began to slowly seep through my body.

"It's all right. I just felt bad about causing Lady Anis and everyone else all this trouble..."

"It can't be helped. It's dangerous for someone from a lower-ranked family to reject a proposal from a higher one."

"...It's so frustrating...," I whispered, despite myself.

What on earth was I supposed to do, then? I felt like crying out.

I didn't want to cause anyone any problems. I was desperate to return the generosity and kindness that everyone had showed me. I didn't want to have to think about anything other than repaying that debt.

"...Frustrating? Yes, I know. You've been enjoying life since coming to the detached palace."

"Ilia...?"

"Lainie, do you mind if I ask you something? Would you be willing to accept a proposal, even if only as a pretense, to free yourself from your current situation? I do think it would be the fastest way."

"...A fake marriage, you mean?" I muttered as I sank into thought.

But it wasn't long before the heavy feeling welling up from deep in my stomach forced me to shake my head.

"...I don't want to accept an engagement proposal, even if just as a pretense. It would only cause the other party unnecessary trouble."

"In that case, it would be ideal if there were no more such proposals in the first place, yes?"

"Indeed. I feel guilty toward my father, but I would sooner continue serving Lady Anis as a maid than return to being a young lady. So I don't even want to think about marriage or engagements."

Was I being selfish? That was just how I wanted to live my life, though. If I could give back to those who helped me, surely I would be able to find happiness and self-satisfaction.

"...There may be a way to help you," Ilia offered.

"Do you have any ideas?"

If there was something I could do, I wanted to know. I turned toward her, and she stared back at me without blinking.

Something about her bearing struck me as a premonition, but I couldn't say of precisely what. Before I could determine its true nature, Ilia spoke up. "You could do the same thing as Lady Anisphia."

"...And what would that be?"

"You could publicly declare that you only have romantic interests in women. Then run around and make sure the whole world hears about it."

"Ah, I see..."

"That would surely reduce the number of men interested in asking for your hand in marriage, and it would make it easier for you to help Lady Anisphia and everyone else here..."

That did sound like a good suggestion. As Ilia had noted, declaring that I was attracted to women would probably keep most men away. Lady Anis herself had proven that.

Nonetheless, some deep-rooted hesitancy prevented me from nodding along in agreement.

"...You don't like that idea?"

"It's not that I don't like it… It's more that, well, I mean…"

Ilia waited patiently for me to find the right words. I exhaled, trying to give form to the stray thoughts swirling around my head.

"…I—I'm no good at anything romantic. I find it all a bit scary."

"…How so?"

"For me, love has kept turning my life upside down. That's why I'm scared of it…"

Indeed, I found it terribly frightening. If the idea of love was all tied up in the right form and shape, it might look something like Lady Anis or Lady Euphyllia. But as wonderful as they were as a couple, even they had crossed paths, clashed, and hurt each other before arriving at the relationship that they had now.

Love and romance offered power—so great that if you took even a single misstep, it could destroy you. I simply couldn't imagine myself being able to properly wield something like that.

And so I held my breath. I didn't want to stand out. I didn't want to be noticed. Even back when I was in the orphanage, and back when my father took me in to be a nobleman's daughter, weak unimposing me was always hiding somewhere, holding my knees as I wept.

"I'm scared. I'm afraid I'll make someone go crazy out of love for me. If it was just friendship, I wouldn't worry so much. But I'm afraid of love. I couldn't stand doing that to someone…"

Having learned to control my vampire powers, I doubted that I would inadvertently compel anyone to like me in that way.

But all it would take was one misstep—one error—and it could happen all over again. *That* was what worried me.

I was afraid. I didn't want to encounter love. I wanted to run off somewhere far away. Romance and affection could grow even from an engagement in name only. Just imagining when my powers might rear their ugly head was enough to turn me away. I couldn't afford to hope for such a thing.

The best that I could do was to watch at a distance. And that was enough for me.

"...As far as I'm concerned, you're a much better person than you seem to think, Lainie."

"I am? Thank you...?"

"I've been watching over you ever since you joined us here at the detached palace. You're neither weak nor irresponsible. But you are sensitive, and you have a gentle heart."

"...Isn't that another way of saying *weak*?"

"If you think being sensitive makes you weak, then that's what it will do. But isn't it your very sensitivity that makes your feelings like beautiful jewels?"

I could feel the heat rising to my cheeks at these words. The bath was already warm, but I was starting to feel even hotter.

"Since coming here, you've grown into an accomplished young woman. You should have more confidence in yourself. I was worried at first when you offered to help Lady Euphyllia, but I also thought it was a good opportunity. Like Lady Anisphia and Lady Euphyllia, you're capable of creating something wonderful."

I was quickly overwhelmed by this praise, twisting my body around as I sank down to my mouth in the hot water.

"Your sensitivity is making you afraid. For you, maybe love is fragile, yet strong and sharply piercing."

"...You might be right," I replied meekly.

Fragile yet strong. That was why it pierced so sharply. Yes—that did sum up my impressions of love rather nicely.

"Which is why if I say this, I'm sure I might end up hurting you."

"...Eh?"

"Lainie...would you like *me* to help?"

For a moment, I couldn't understand what she had just said. No— even after a moment, I *still* failed to understand. Nor did I want to. Yet Ilia's words echoed in my ears again and again.

I could only stare back at her. Her expression was clearer than usual. But why? Why couldn't I shake the feeling that that expression of hers wasn't something that she would show in her usual state?

My throat was dry, parched. With an audible gulp, I threw out a question of my own: "Ilia, what do you—?"

"You're special to me. As my understudy, as a colleague—as a person."

"…You're lying."

"It's no lie. These are my true feelings… Your situation won't change unless you do something to change it. I know that you don't want to trouble anyone. I can imagine how painful it must be for you to talk about romance and love, considering your powers and your past. So I wanted to tell you how *I* feel."

"Wh-why…?" I murmured.

In my confusion, that was the only word I could manage. Before I knew it, Ilia reached out to my cheek—and as her fingers touched my skin, my whole body trembled.

"I couldn't bear to lose it," she said to me.

"Lose what…?"

"You seemed so happy when you came here, Lainie. You took all my lessons to heart and attended to Lady Anisphia and the others with a beaming smile. Even with your painful past, I found something of immense value in your smile—and that, I couldn't bear to lose."

Ilia's fingers—the only things that I could now grasp—were hotter than anything else.

"Will you take me as your partner, Lainie?"

Accepting Ilia as my lover to turn down the engagement proposals… It might work. But while I could clearly recognize the solution, I felt pressure building up inside me that was starting to make me sick.

"…That won't… Wh-what are you suggesting…? You like *me*? Y-you're lying…"

"Lainie…"

"You've fallen under my enchantment powers! Th-that's not love…!"

This couldn't possibly be her true self speaking. It couldn't be.

Right. This was a fake seed that I had planted. It was strange, it was wrong, it was—

Ah, h-have I done it again...?

My vision went dark. Could I have compelled someone to fall in love with me for my own protection? And not just anyone—Ilia, who had offered me guidance, who had taught me so much.

Just as my confusion was about to get the better of me, Ilia tugged at my hand. I was more flustered than I thought; my body leaned against hers. The *thump-thump* of her heartbeat rang in my ears.

"...Are you feeling dizzy? I brought this up in the wrong place."

"Ilia, I—"

"Let's get out of the bath. We can calm down first before we continue this conversation."

Continue this conversation? Whatever for? Was that really necessary...? No, maybe it was. I had to apologize, to make amends.

"I'm...sorry."

"Lainie?"

"I...slipped up again... I'm sorry. I'm sorry. I'm sorry...!"

I had repeated my sins all over again. My heart felt as though it had been ripped from my chest, leaving me in so much pain that I wanted to die.

So all I could do was apologize, over and over again. Why couldn't I change? Why was I this weak?

I was so saddened by this grim reality that all I could do was keep cursing myself.

* * *

The next day, I found myself laid up hopelessly in bed. My head was foggy, my body inexplicably languid. I also had a tickle in my throat and was coughing occasionally.

Sitting by my side was Lady Tilty, staring down at me with her brow furrowed in a grim expression.

"You caught a cold from the hot water," she said. "You're a nuisance, you know that? Anis dragged me here because you've got a fever. And so early in the morning!"

"I'm...sorry..."

Given my vampiric condition, the number of doctors capable of examining me was extremely limited. That being the case, I couldn't thank Lady Tilty enough for coming on such short notice.

But somewhere in my heart, a deep stagnation was building up. Ah, here I was making another nuisance of myself.

"You were talking to Ilia in the bath for quite some time, I hear. It's not like her to make such a silly blunder..."

"...It's...my fault. She didn't—"

"Ilia told me everything. I don't know what she was thinking, taking her iron mask off then and there, but she was out of line confessing to you in a place like that."

"She told you everything?!" I blurted out.

I couldn't believe it. So everyone knew? Had I driven her mad? I was about to be overwhelmed by despair.

Tilty snorted derisively. "You're a disaster, too. Goodness."

"...Um, Lady Tilty?"

"What?"

"I... Have I done it again...? Did I bewitch Ilia without even realizing...?" I asked in a trembling voice.

Tilty's eyes widened with shock. She started sulking, and I could even sense a tinge of anger from her.

"Lainie," she began.

"Y-yes...?"

"You didn't do anything. Enough with these silly delusions."

"B-but—!"

"You're in control of your powers. You aren't going around triggering them at random. If you think stress or confusion or weakness is capable of activating them, then why haven't *I* felt the effects? And even if they did activate involuntarily, the impact would only be mild attraction, not total control."

Her sharp, reproachful remarks left me feeling like a blade had just been thrust down my throat. She really was angry with me.

"If that's what you think, Ilia's feelings will go unanswered. Now, enough with this ridiculous misconception of yours."

"...But she said she *likes* me."

"Hah? Are you trying to say you used your abilities on her without realizing it? How stupid are you?" Tilty snorted dismissively. "It's true, I can't say that we've fully elucidated your powers. And you're capable of more than you were before, so it's possible that your defensive reactions have increased in potency, too. But they're not absolute. In fact, right now, I'm so mad that I want to slap you right across the face. And yet you aren't defending yourself; you're not trying to charm me. I can say that with surety."

Tilty spoke flatly, her voice barely containing her anger as she all but pushed me away. "Right now, you're doubting yourself. And because of that, I'm here to examine you, while Ilia, who cares so much about you, has you constantly on her mind. Anis and Euphyllia are fretting about you, too. Are you calling all of that into question? Do try to be more aware, please."

"No...I didn't mean that!"

"That's why I'm telling you—enough with these ridiculous assumptions. I was taken aback by Ilia's blind naïveté, but I'm even more appalled by your misconceptions. *I* deserve an apology for being dragged into all this."

"...I'm sorry."

"Do you really think words will be enough to resolve this?"

"Eh...?"

I didn't know what to do. She had asked me to apologize, but then she went on to criticize me for doing just that.

Lady Tilty said that I was mistaken, that I hadn't forced anyone to fall in love with me. Then did Ilia really mean it when she said that she liked me...?

"...No, Ilia, she must have seen how I was struggling. She just said it out of concern for me..."

"Are you trying to insult her, Lainie?"

"I—I'm not insulting her!"

"What you're saying is that no one could possibly like you. Ilia told you she does, but are you suggesting you don't believe her, that you don't trust her?"

"No! I don't *not* trust her! But there's no need for her to put me first!"

"Why not?"

"Why not...? I mean..."

Because her responsibility was to always put Lady Anis first.

I knew just how much Ilia cherished Lady Anis. That's why Ilia's special someone couldn't be anyone else. I couldn't possibly take Lady Anis's place.

Yet I couldn't put those nebulous feelings into words. *Why?* I asked myself, but no answer was forthcoming.

I fell silent, and Tilty turned her back to me from her position on the edge of the bed.

"You're having silly thoughts again," she told me. "Although if you ask me, Ilia is partly to blame here, too, for her bad timing, her clumsiness, and her poor understanding of her own feelings."

"Ilia...did nothing wrong..."

"...True, Ilia has done nothing wrong. And neither have you, Lainie."

"But—but I've caused her so much trouble, and now I've driven her to madness..."

"Indeed, which is why she isn't at fault. But you're also mistaken on that point. Yes, she has gone crazy; there's no doubt about that."

I had no idea what Lady Tilty was saying. When I looked up and glanced toward her, only her face was turned my way.

"How well do you know Ilia? Do you understand just how mad that woman is?"

"...I'm afraid I don't follow."

"She was an irredeemable fool up until Lady Euphyllia came along, and it only got worse when you arrived," Lady Tilty said with a snort as she stared into the distance. Her tone of voice was almost spiteful, but I could hear the pity behind her words.

After a moment, she glanced toward the entrance. "If you want to know more, why don't you ask the princess eavesdropping from behind the door?"

"...Er, I didn't think the mood was right to come inside, that's all," Lady Anis said as she stepped inside, fixing Lady Tilty with a dissatisfied glare.

With that, Lady Tilty rose to her feet and made for the exit, patting Lady Anis on the shoulder as she passed her by. "Physically, she's fine. I didn't come here to be her counselor, so I'll leave the rest to you."

"Thank you, Tilty."

"Don't drag me into any more unnecessary quarrels, you hear?"

With those words, she closed the door behind her, leaving me and Lady Anis alone.

Feeling a new surge of guilt rising up inside me, I hastened to make a fresh apology. "I'm so very sorry, Lady Anis."

"It's all right. My work can wait. I'm more worried about you," she said, taking a seat at the edge of the bed, where Lady Tilty had been sitting a moment earlier.

I didn't want her to see my face right now, so I was secretly grateful that she sat with her back to me.

And yet, with Lady Anis by my side, my deepest-held feelings slowly rose to the surface.

"...I..."

"Yes?"

"I—I hate myself... It hurts so much... I just want to disappear... I want to give back, but all I ever do is cause trouble... I can't do it... I'm afraid, and I hate myself for it..."

I halted and stammered, unable to get the words out properly. I knew I was being incoherent, that none of it made any sense. I couldn't even understand myself.

"Hmm."

Still, Lady Anis nodded along, listening to me in silence. She didn't look my way, but she was definitely there, lending me her ear.

"I...I don't...know what to do anymore..."

"...Ilia told me what happened yesterday."

My body froze as Lady Anis spoke. I stared at the floor, and my body trembled under an icy chill.

"Lainie. Lift your head," Lady Anis said in a calming voice.

Unable to hold back my tears, I gritted my teeth and looked up.

Lady Anis's expression was happy but at the same time troubled and conflicted. I didn't know why she was looking at me like that, and I was growing even more confused.

"First of all, Lainie, calm down. Let's take a deep, slow breath," she said, patting me softly on the back.

I noticed my raised hand was shaking slightly. With her free hand, Lady Anis took hold of it, clutching it warmly while she patted me on the back until I had calmed down. As she instructed, I did my best to control my breathing.

"Are you relaxed now?"

"...Yes. I'm...sorry..."

"Good. Well then, why don't we have a talk?"

"...?"

"You know, Lainie, I don't really know how to feel right now myself. Should I be surprised? Happy? Lonely? I would never have expected this from Ilia. But it's good news, don't you think?"

"Eh...?"

I sat there dumbfounded, not sure what to make of all this. Good news? What was good news exactly?

"Lainie, maybe you think Ilia only fell in love with you because of your vampire powers, no? That you cursed her, perhaps? But even if that was the case, I don't think it's a bad thing. It might actually be for the best."

"Why...? Why would you say that...?"

"Ilia isn't very tenacious, you know?" Lady Anis murmured sadly. Her voice was weak, as though she was at a loss, on the verge of giving up. "I wonder if she's only recently come to terms with it all. She's a little crazy, right? That's because she wasn't properly loved while growing up. I think her relationship with me is partly to blame, too. We never interacted with a great many people, so we lived our lives without worrying about others."

"…She called herself wretched…"

"I'm the one who did that to her," Lady Anis said with self-directed scorn. As she glanced down at the floor, her gaze seemed somewhat pained. "Do you know about her upbringing and her family? Her parents treated her as little more than a political pawn, a puppet to control however they liked."

"…She did tell me about that once."

"I see. I don't regret bringing her here as my personal attendant. If I did, that would only serve to make her angry. But I can't change the fact that I left her somewhat warped, and I never did anything to fix it."

"…B-but what *could* you have done about it?"

"Exactly. You can't change the past. And I'm sure I would make the same choices again if offered the chance," Lady Anis said without the slightest hesitation. "I can't give up on her, and I can't bend on my other interests. I can't change her, either. That's the kind of relationship we have."

She gave me a soft smile—one that came from the bottom of her heart. She really believed she had nothing to feel ashamed of.

"We both thought we would be all right if we didn't change, so we didn't try to seek any more than we already had. It was enough that we enjoyed each other's company, that we could live in the same place without suffocating the other."

Lady Anis patted her chest as she spoke, carefully listing each important point one by one.

"But then I met Euphie, and she met you. Our relationship might not have changed, but those with the people around us have. And they'll lead us to find changes in ourselves. There's a certain sadness in change, but it's inevitable, and we should welcome it with joy. No matter how it happened, I'm truly happy, I really am, that Ilia has fallen in love with someone... I can protect her by myself, but I can't change her."

"Lady Anis..."

"Otherwise, we would end up losing the relationship that we already have without ever leaving a real impact on the other. I'm afraid of that, and I'm sure she wouldn't want it, either. Because we were each other's closest partner, you know? So we were most comfortable in each other's company. That was all that mattered, nothing more."

All of a sudden, Lady Anis reached out to hug me, holding my head in her arms. Though caught by surprise, I didn't resist. With my ear pressed up against her chest, I could hear the steady rhythm of her heart beating.

"It's nice to have a relaxed relationship, one where you spoil each other. But if you do that, it can't go anywhere further, and it can never change—because there's no need for it to. I'm happy I've gotten close to Euphie, but I was really worried about Ilia. I want her to be able to change, too."

"...Really?"

"Yeah. I was relieved when she took an interest in you. She seemed to be having so much fun looking out for you. As far as I'm concerned, any relationship is fine so long as it offers her room to grow."

"...Even if she was bewitched by a vampire into falling in love with her?"

"I don't think she would have been able to grow otherwise. And if she didn't grow, she would have stayed the way she was forever. She would stick by my side, showing me respect and affection, but we wouldn't be able to move anywhere beyond that. She wouldn't seek out any opportunities to grow as a person... And that would just be too lonely, too sad."

"Lonely...? Sad...?"

"I'm here now because of Euphie, because she sought me out. Thanks to her, I'm chasing after the dreams that I was about to throw away, even though deep inside I couldn't do it. So I wish Ilia had someone like that, too. And I would be so happy if it was you, Lainie."

"But that's...not what she wanted... Is it?"

"Did you decide that for yourself, Lainie?" Lady Anis asked. The scolding tone in her voice caused me to flinch.

She grabbed me by the shoulders to lift me up and push me slightly away, then she turned around, her eyes blazing. I was almost overwhelmed; I wanted to look away.

"It's not like I don't understand why you're afraid, Lainie. I know you've convinced yourself that you're responsible for this. But still, I have to tell you: Don't turn your back on her."

"Turn my back on her...?"

"I was wondering whether I should say something to you—something about taking a bold new step. Ilia would never ask me for advice. She wouldn't ask Euphie, either. She would never rely on someone else... She can't." Lady Anis's voice was somber.

My voice caught in my throat just listening.

"I think it's wonderful she spoke up about what she wanted. It wasn't required of her as part of her official duties, and she wasn't obligated to do it. So even if you don't share her feelings, I don't want you to disrespect that."

"...But, Lady Anis, I..."

"I understand you're afraid of your powers. And you know, I think it's good you feel that way. But don't forget—your situation is just like my magicology. What matters is how you use them. And you helped Ilia start moving forward. I was surprised and happy to see her take that first step." Lady Anis spoke as though in prayer, her voice infinitely gentle, readily calling to mind the fullness of her feelings for Ilia. I could see that she cared about her deeply.

"I can't tell you to accept her feelings," she continued. "But don't turn your back on them. If you need time, tell her so. If you don't feel the same way, tell her. Silence would be the cruelest response of all... But if you can accept her, even just a little bit, I want you to help her move forward."

"...What kind of person is Ilia to you, Lady Anis?" I asked without thinking.

With that, she flashed me an awkward smile. After letting out a brief groan, she finally responded: "That's a difficult question... I guess the easiest way to put it is we're master and servant. I think of her as family, although I can't really put our relationship into words. But in any case, she's very important to me."

"...And what do you think of *me*, bewitching her with my powers?"

"Hmm. I don't really know. I mean, it's beyond human control. But if your abilities caused her to feel something for someone other than me, for her to fall in love...then maybe that has me a little frustrated."

I stared back wide-eyed at this surprise confession. I wasn't expecting her to use the word *frustrated*, and I was unable to respond.

"It isn't quite jealousy, and maybe *frustration* isn't exactly the right word, either. But if I had to find words, *frustrated* is what comes to mind... Probably because she's been by my side for so long. And now she's moving away from me, little by little. So I'm frustrated and a little bit sad—but also incredibly happy for her."

She spoke like a child showing off her treasures, her smile so endearing that I couldn't take my eyes off her.

I couldn't find any single word to describe it. But in her face, I could see it all—her inner nobility.

Lady Anis sincerely cared about Ilia and wished for her happiness, but she could nudge her forward only from behind—as though to say that *I* should be the one to accept her.

I still couldn't accept that fact for what it was.

"...Lady Anis...I—I feel like I'm going to drown. It's suffocating. And terrifying. Even if I can find happiness, I don't know whether I'll be able to keep it... That's what I'm afraid of... I'm petrified...!"

It had been excruciating for so long now—like I was struggling just to keep my head above water each and every day.

I was so happy when I came here, really I was. I wanted to spend all my time living in this new life that I had found.

Losing this newfound happiness was what I feared most. I trembled, hunkered down, and wanted to push it all away from me.

"It's all right," Lady Anis called out as though to console me, her words imbued with strength. "I can see that you're scared. Even if you're helpless like me, you won't just leave it at that. I'm sure of it. You won't leave yourself or those you care about to drown. But you mustn't forget, there are people here who will lend you a helping hand if you just speak up."

Then, holding me close, she asked a question that struck to the very heart of the matter: "Is Ilia…someone you want help with?"

* * *

A few hours had passed since Lady Anis had left my room after calming me down, when a knock at my door woke me from my state of half sleep.

"Lainie, it's me. May I come in?"

It was Ilia's voice. As I snapped awake, my mind began to clear. I took one deep breath, then another, before answering, "Come in…"

"Pardon me," she said, stepping inside.

Before I knew it, I startled—taken aback by the sight of dark circles under her eyes.

"Is this a good time?" she asked.

"It's all right… Um, Ilia? You look really tired. Is this a good time for *you*?"

"I couldn't sleep last night. But physically, I'm fine. More importantly, are you? I'm terribly sorry for burdening you with such a long conversation last night."

"You don't need to apologize… I won't know how to respond."

"…I see. Shall I make some tea?"

"If it's no trouble."

If we were going to talk, it would be best to do so over a relaxing drink. As I listened to her putting everything together, I closed my eyes to gather my thoughts.

Soon, Ilia placed a teacup on the side table. I sat up, brought the cup to my lips, and took a sip.

Maybe this was because I was so thirsty, but it tasted particularly nice. It brought back a wave of nostalgic memories, and I felt the muscles around my mouth relax.

"...I love your tea, Ilia," I said.

"I'm so glad to hear you say that."

"It's true. I'm so happy. Lady Anis is so kind to me, and Lady Euphyllia let me stay here at the detached palace. I was so worried, but I can still remember my relief when it all worked out."

A moment of silence passed between us before finally Ilia spoke up. "Again, I apologize for last night... In hindsight, I was too abrupt."

"No... I was just surprised."

"...If I've made a nuisance of myself, please disregard what I said as idle nonsense."

"You're not a nuisance!" I responded forcefully, my voice louder than I had intended.

Ilia's eyes widened a little; she seemed ready to jump to her feet with worry.

"I'm sorry for shouting... I don't think you're a nuisance. But I was stunned, and I couldn't come to a decision right away..."

"That's only natural... I couldn't imagine for myself how the conversation ought to go, so I ended up just telling you how I feel. I'm to blame for not considering the burden you're carrying."

"...Ilia—did you come out with that proposal because you feel sorry for me?" I asked, doing my utmost to keep my voice from quavering.

At that moment, she flashed me a faint smile—a fleeting expression that could fade at any moment, fully imparting her sense of unease.

"If that was how you took it...perhaps you're right."

"...You don't deny it?"

"I'm confused myself—I can't even understand my own feelings. I'm racking my brain looking for the answer. I don't know what to do, and I don't want to force you into anything."

In essence, her true, unadulterated intention had simply been to lay out her feelings, without having given much thought to her words.

Hearing all this, how exactly did I feel...? She and I may have been different people, but I knew what it meant not to understand one's own emotions.

It was so heartrending—like I was drowning and couldn't breathe. My body shook, and I had to struggle to keep my teeth from clattering against each other.

I grabbed my arm to hide my trembling, digging my nails into my skin. The pain helped calm my nerves a little. To be honest, I doubted that I could trust the goodwill of others to such an extent.

But that didn't mean that I could run away without facing it. Still, I was terrified to tell her the wish lurking inside me.

"...Lainie, you don't have to force yourself."

My eyes widened at the sound of her soothing voice. That wasn't the Ilia I knew.

I'd never seen her look like this—she had a lonely smile that was gentle despite the pain. My chest tightened in alarm.

No! I didn't want to put this expression on her face...!

"I know I've burdened you with all this. It's enough for me that you know how I feel. I really am sorry...for making you worry so."

"...W-wait! It's my fault...! I was just so scared, I couldn't bring myself to believe it...! You're not in the wrong, Ilia!"

"No. I should have kept my silence rather than burden you."

"I...! I'm only this worried because I'm so happy right now!"

I lost my temper and shouted at the top of my lungs.

Ilia's composure faltered; she blinked again and again.

Watching on, I felt the smallest upswell of irrational anger toward her, and unable to quell my crumbling emotions, I glared at her.

"How could I *not* hate the idea of us becoming lovers just for my benefit?! Why won't you understand?! You know what kind of monster I am! You know what I did to you! So how can you say that you'll accept me?! That you're hoping for something...?!"

"...Lainie?"

"I've been betrayed by expectations all my life! Even if you say you love me, you'll curse me for betraying you! Everyone always blames me! It's always my fault in the end! I want to trust people! I want them to like me how they might like anyone else. I don't want to be special, but everyone always goes and forces me to *be* special! And then in the end, they blame me for it all!"

Even when I was an orphan, even after becoming a nobleman's daughter: People always claimed to like me, but then they acted as though I had betrayed them when I failed to live up to their expectations.

So I had learned—that I couldn't afford to love.

The only person I let myself love was my mother. My happiest memories were of her. And in my memories, she would always be the same, so it didn't matter how special I made her.

Even when my father took me in and gave me a place of my own, I didn't fit in right away. And life at the Aristocratic Academy was no better than life at the orphanage.

To me, it was a wonderful thing simply not to be at risk of starving. I knew that, but in my heart I was always frightened, rejecting everything and always giving up.

"Lady Anis showed me the way. Lady Euphyllia offered me forgiveness. And you taught me how to live! That's enough! I have to do something more...! I can't keep relying on everyone! I can't...!"

I didn't want people showering me with kindness. Once that happened, I would be forever trapped.

I knew for a fact that I wasn't strong. I couldn't be like Lady Anis or Lady Euphyllia.

But at the very least, I didn't want to get in everyone's way. If at all possible, I would be overjoyed to support them, to have their backs for once. But I couldn't do that. Not only was I failing to help them, I was dragging them down. And that only left me feeling miserable and helpless.

"Can you really accept me like this...? It's just pity, what you're feeling, isn't it...? You feel sorry for me, that's all..."

"Lainie."

Before I knew it, tears were streaming down my cheeks; my voice faltered as I wept.

Seeing me like that, Ilia stood up from her seat and placed her forehead against mine, then lifted a hand to my cheek and wiped away my tears.

"*I'm* the monster, Lainie. I took comfort in being accepted by Lady Anisphia's side. Because doing so suited my own convenience. But you're different. You came here of your own volition. You wanted to stay by my side; you wanted to be useful. I learned that from your charms. You've given me something that I can't earn just by serving... You've soothed my heart."

"Ilia..."

"Maybe everyone has these feelings, but I failed to understand them. I was lacking, as a human being. But you taught me to feel, and thanks to you, I was able to grow, little by little. Watching you showed me what it meant to grow, what the next step would be. I could feel the meaning behind everything that I had accumulated over the years. *You're* the one who made me realize all that."

Ilia spoke as though offering solace, struggling to convey the hidden meaning that she had found in my coming here.

"I've learned so much through you. Your humanity, the way you're always so considerate of others, the way you're always trying to move forward, no matter how frightened you might be. I want to help you, because I love the way you always give everything your best. I would love nothing more than for us to continue serving Lady Anisphia and Lady Euphyllia together. That's why I want to protect you, to shield you from anything that might stand in your way."

She paused there, pulling her forehead away as she stared straight into my eyes. My lips were pursed tightly, and I found myself averting my gaze.

"...I *am* a vampire, you know...?"

"I know."

"If we become lovers, I'll end up making you *special*, though?"

"I don't mind."

"I'll want to drink lots of your blood, and I'll end up hurting you. It will be one selfish act after another."

"I'll do my best to help you however I can."

"I...don't know what I'll do next time someone betrays me..."

"...Do you think *I'll* turn on you, Lainie?" Ilia asked, her voice sinking a little.

I shook my head. "I...I'm afraid of being selfish. I don't want to lose anything anymore..."

"Then I'll do my best not to make you anxious."

"...I'll ask you which of us is more important to you, me or Lady Anis."

Ilia scowled. After a short moment, she let out a groan before finally speaking up: "Why would you do such a thing...?"

"You wouldn't choose me?"

"...I see. Your selfishness *can* be rather difficult."

"...That's right. I don't exactly have the nicest of personalities."

Ilia raised her eyebrows in consternation, then quickly exhaled and pulled me into a hug. Caught in her sudden embrace, I found myself settling into her arms.

"But you wouldn't be happy if I chose you in response to that question, Lainie."

"...Why do you think that?"

"Because you care about Lady Anisphia and Lady Euphyllia and a great many others, too. That's why you can't prioritize yourself, isn't it? If I chose you, you would feel like you had forced me to do so, yes?"

Now that she'd pointed this out, I realized that I couldn't breathe, tears welling up in my eyes as my throat constricted. I couldn't deny it. I'd imagined the exact same scenario as she had.

"So please don't ask questions like that, as though you're testing me."

"...Ilia."

"Don't compare your worth with that of others, Lainie. You're fine as yourself. You don't have to impose justifications or value judgments on yourself. So long as you remain yourself, I'll follow you anywhere. I won't hesitate to protect you. So please, let me."

With those words, Ilia released me from her embrace and placed her hands on my shoulders. Then, her face drew near to mine...and our lips met in a gentle kiss.

By the time I let out a weak sigh, I realized what she had done, and my body stiffened. And yet...I didn't mind.

Again and again, Ilia pecked at me, and I kissed her back. Each time we touched, a bolt of lightning ran down my spine, numbing me and sapping my strength.

Just as I was about to descend into the dreamiest of states, my last remaining vestiges of logic caused me to resist. I placed a hand on Ilia's chest and gently pushed her away.

"Ilia, why did you...kiss me?!"

"I promised to protect you, but I know you won't believe me deep down. So I thought teaching your body to react would be faster. In fact, you've always learned more quickly by example."

"But that doesn't mean—!"

"You don't like it?" she asked.

I felt my cheeks heating up in response to that question. I didn't *dis*like it. But I was too embarrassed to actually admit that.

I didn't mind being kissed—in fact, I had practically already accepted it. It made me so happy that she thought of me this way. But at the same time, I was still scared.

If I lost myself in this warmth, it would all be over. That was why my body was trying to resist. Yet a part of me didn't want to resist. My mind was contradicting itself, leaving me caught in a rut.

"Stop... W-wait! Wait, please! We can't do this, Ilia...!"

"What can't we do? Tell me clearly."

"I—I mean...k-kissing..."

"Why not? Because you don't want me to?"

"Th-that isn't it...! I—I can't do it!"

"I know that."

"Eh?!"

Ilia narrowed her eyes like a cat, the corners of her lips rising in a grin—and as she did so, an icy chill coursed down my spine.

"I thought you weren't happy with having me as your partner, but it seems I was mistaken. In that case, I can only conclude that the point of failure lies with you. As your teacher, it's my job to give you a thorough education."

"E-education...? B-but that's a separate matter!"

"Then convince me. Give me reason to trust your word."

The bed creaked under our weight as Ilia covered me from above, staring down at my face.

With her on top, I couldn't resist. She had the same glint in her eyes as when she was instructing me. What was worse, I knew this was my fault, leaving me even more frozen.

"Now then, let's start today's lesson. Our goal is to discover what we want to be. We have plenty of time, so let's talk until we're both convinced, Lainie."

* * *

"...Um, look—I'm glad you two talked things out," I began, "but why is Lainie curled up on the bed like a caterpillar?"

"This is the result of a mutually satisfactory discussion, Lady Anisphia," Ilia explained.

She'd gone to check up on Lainie and was now casually rebuffing my questions. What, exactly, was I supposed to make of that?

I stole a glance at the bundle of bedsheets, still trembling visibly from across the room.

"Uh-huh... And then what?"

"We decided to enter a trial relationship to see how things go."

"A trial relationship," I repeated despite myself.

What's that *supposed to mean?*

"These emotions have me a bit in over my head," Ilia continued.

"Lainie similarly wants to explore her feelings, so we agreed to take our time and see what develops."

"R-right... But why is she curled up like a caterpillar, then?" I asked.

"A partner requires pampering, as I understand."

The bundled mass of bedding shook once more. *Seriously, what did Ilia do?* I wondered, glancing at her face—and she offered me a gentle smile like a flower blooming, her grin so dazzling that it made me do a double take.

To be honest, I didn't have the faintest idea how this was going to work out, but I was relieved to learn that nothing bad had happened.

After that, I made my way outside, while Lainie remained in Ilia's care. Best to leave them both alone for now.

I might as well cook dinner tonight instead. Euphie would be hungry when she got back.

She may have lost her attachment to food after becoming a spirit covenantor, but her body would break down without any physical nourishment.

"Lainie is recovering, too, so maybe something light. Bread and soup and..."

As I debated a possible menu, I wondered what kind of face Euphie would make on her return. Would she be surprised, or exasperated?

It was fun to imagine her response. Deep down, I felt the smallest bit—only a smidgen—of sadness, but on the whole, I was ecstatic. And before I knew it, those feelings began to overflow, pouring out as I spoke:

"I'm so happy for you, Ilia. Thank you, Lainie."

INTERLUDE
Like a Ripple Expanding

Viscount Nebels's residence—my parents' home—was located in a corner of a precinct in the royal capital lined with the mansions of various aristocrats.

I, Halphys Nebels, was facing a memo board in my room as I finished up the documents, and once everything was done and dusted, I took a sip of my tea.

It was already lukewarm: a firm reminder of just how preoccupied I had been with my work.

"Maybe I should brew a fresh pot..."

My whole body was stiff from having been sitting so long. Just as I was about to call for someone, there came a knock at my door—followed by the voice of the butler, who had been serving my family now for generations.

"Are you all right, milady?"

"Yes. Is something wrong?"

"Master Marion is here to pay you a visit..."

"Marion?!"

I leaped to my feet in surprise. There were no plans for my fiancé to visit today, so this really was out of the blue.

I looked myself over once more. I hadn't expected to see anyone, so I was dressed in rather plain garb.

"Tell him I'll be right there. And could you provide me a change of clothes?"

"I've already seen to it."

No sooner had the butler finished his announcement than several maids entered the room, helping me get ready as I calmed my racing heart.

Marion had been so busy lately, making it somewhat difficult for us to find the time to meet like this. Still, I felt a surge of joy that he had taken the opportunity to visit, along with a sense of guilt in equal proportion.

Hoping to shake off all these complicated emotions, once I was finished getting ready, I made my way briskly to the parlor, where Marion was waiting for me.

"Thank you for waiting, Marion."

"Hey, Halphys. I'm sorry for dropping in on such short notice, but I was hoping you would be able to make time for tea."

"I'm honored that you took the time to visit."

He approached my side with a gentle smile. My face was about to soften in response to that perennial kindness, so I had to scold it into a ladylike composure.

After letting him escort me to my seat, we soon found ourselves sitting across from one another. A maid delivered tea and sweets, offered us a polite bow, and then retreated to a corner of the room.

"Sorry for not being able to come sooner, Halphys," Marion told me.

"No, I understand how busy you are, Master Marion, and the Ministry of the Arcane is going through a difficult time. You needn't worry about me."

"If this isn't a right old mess! I'm not sure I'm comfortable with the idea of falling out of your affections on account of my work," Marion said, his brow creased in a troubled frown as he offered up another friendly smile.

I felt my chest tighten as I took in that expression. Was he just feigning composure while about to break down? I couldn't be sure.

"...I'm really sorry," he continued. "I know I'm putting you through plenty of trouble."

"Not in the slightest," I answered.

"I'm aware that certain people are trying to interfere with our engagement. Some have been reaching out to me, others to you."

"...Marion."

Unsure what else to say, I could offer him only a troubled look. I watched as his face tensed up. He stared straight back at me.

"Let me begin by saying that there is no intention on my part of canceling our engagement. I won't give you up unless you yourself insist on it. Please remember that."

"...Are you sure you want to say that? There may be good potential matches for you other than me."

After all, our engagement had been entered into solely because our families were on good terms with one another—and my parents, without a son of their own, had decided to welcome him as a son-in-law. So for both houses, the engagement was neither a remedy nor a poison, so to speak.

However, the situation had changed following the fall of Count Chartreuse, the former director of the Ministry of the Arcane. Considering the position of Count Antti's family, I couldn't help but conclude that he could make a much better match than being groomed by a humble viscount's daughter.

"Halphys, do you see our relationship as merely a means to establishing family connections? I'm more than that, you know..."

"You haven't done anything wrong, Marion! Our engagement may be for our families' benefit, but I adore you on a personal level, too!"

"Then enough with these unhappy words. I haven't failed so badly as to make you talk that way. I know I'm making this difficult for you, but I still want to be with you. If I didn't, I wouldn't have made the time to come here."

"...I'm sorry. I don't doubt your feelings, Marion. But I just can't help worrying that I'm ruining your prospects because of my inadequacies."

Marion was a potential future director of the Ministry of the Arcane, whereas I was just an ordinary viscount's daughter. My skills at magic were nothing exceptional, and my appearance was rather plain, too. I'd lost count of how many times I had rued my lack of charm.

…But still, I couldn't give up, either. Because I loved him, too.

"…Inadequacies…? Do you fail to recognize your own successes?"

"Huh?"

"Your reputation has been on the rise lately for your contributions in building that new magical tool with Princess Anisphia."

"The Thought Board, you mean? That was Her Highness's idea. I just helped out with it."

"Princess Euphyllia has been telling everyone that the end product was partly thanks to your input as well. And that Princess Anisphia spoke very highly of your suggestions. She apparently said that you have a great many ideas, and that she would like to keep you in her employ to borrow your insights."

"Princess Anisphia said that…?"

She certainly was an especially friendly person, and not one to hold back with her praise, but I had no idea that she had been telling others about me.

"I also heard that you handled the petitions from the various departments for the distribution of Thought Boards, Halphys. Thanks to that, the preliminary evaluation is proceeding very well indeed. You've done a great job."

"I'm honored. But that was all I could really do…"

"And didn't you prepare a document outlining how to start introducing these Thought Boards into people's workflows? Princess Euphyllia spoke very highly of it. You've been given an important job by Princess Anisphia, and you've established a solid position for yourself. Take pride in what you've done. I'm happy for you, too."

Embarrassed by these words of praise, I lifted my teacup to my mouth and took a sip. Marion, meanwhile, kept watching behind that smile of his.

"You're very modest, Halphys. But if it should come to pass, I would love for you to support me in my work as well. Rather, perhaps I should attend to Princess Anisphia, too?"

"Wh-what are you saying? You're an honored member of the Ministry of the Arcane, Marion!"

"When I see Princess Anisphia, I sometimes wonder whether my sense of pride isn't misplaced," he said with a sigh as he looked off into the distance. "I've had a great many opportunities to hear about her from Princess Euphyllia, but it was her comments on the historical documents kept at the ministry that left me particularly shocked. Apparently, Princess Anisphia felt that the phrasing was overly ornate, making it difficult to grasp the actual situation described at times. Have you heard about that, Halphys?"

"Yes. I was there during that discussion."

"As far as we nobles are concerned, it perhaps goes without thinking. Rather, we study precisely so that we can read."

"...But that's just the aristocracy."

"Did you have any thoughts on the topic, Halphys?"

"I've come to feel more strongly about magical tools since being given the opportunity help produce them. But I can see how the writing style with which we are familiar came into being because it was produced by those who can wield magic—after all, in order to control magic, we need to pray to spirits to enhance our mental images. But commoners aren't exposed to this. They don't need long texts to enhance their imaginations."

That was why, when offering explanations to commoners, nobles tended to limit their expressions and use simple, easy-to-understand words—though many nobles might well consider such sentences embarrassingly elementary. Exercising complicated phraseology, and then deciphering it later, was part of what made one a noble.

Then again, if you were to ask me whether I considered simple documents vulgar, I would have to say no. For us in the aristocracy, it came as a matter of course, but from the point of view of the common folk, it was nothing more than useless ostentation. It was a disconnect in values.

"All this time, historical materials have been read exclusively by the aristocracy, because no one else has had any need to read them," I explained. "As such, there was never any need to correct the materials stored at the Ministry of the Arcane. However, I believe that assumption will be called into question from now on."

"Essentially, as magical tools become more widespread, the lives of the common people will change, too." Marion nodded along in agreement, his expression serious. "We nobles with the ability to wield magic may no longer be absolute. It's very much conceivable that a commoner elevated to the peerage may be given a high position overseeing the affairs of the realm. Should that happen, I wonder if our materials will suffice in their current state."

In conclusion, it wasn't essential for non-mages to be educated to read and understand documents that were written under the assumption that they would be read by mages.

Of course, it would be better if non-mages *could* read them—it just wouldn't be essential.

As such, there were arguments to be made for both positions as to whether the documents should be updated to make it easier to source information.

"It goes without saying, but the simpler a document's writing style, the easier it will be to read—and to have written in the first place. I doubt it will be necessary to adapt every form of document, but perhaps we should consider some, given the current situation."

"Princess Anisphia said something similar, that she would like us to edit the texts in the necessary areas and then re-archive them."

"The princess is familiar with the lives and the perspectives of the common classes. Their viewpoints are rather different from those of ordinary nobles. In the future, I suspect that those capable of thinking flexibly in a changing country will rise to high stations... I doubt the authority figures who have held real power at the ministry all this time will be able to cope with this new reality."

"…Marion."

"Princesses Euphyllia and Anisphia are both giving this all their effort. If anyone was to try to oppose them, I don't think it would end in their favor… But even so, some people simply can't change." He paused there, letting out an exhausted sigh.

I had known that the Ministry of the Arcane was in turmoil, but might things be even worse there than I had thought?

"I'm not completely satisfied with it all, either. Of course, if someone came to me saying that everything we've been doing all this time is wrong and ordered me to change it all, I don't think I would be able to just accept it. But at the same time, it would be folly to set yourself up against either princess out of your own resistance to change."

"…Yes, that's true. Besides, Princess Anisphia doesn't want to deal with the Ministry of the Arcane, either."

"I can understand them being concerned about maintaining their prestigious positions, but it's something else entirely when your concern for prestige stops you from doing what needs to be done. They just never stop to think."

"Indeed, I feel the same way. As a noble in this country, I think each and every one of us ought to consider how we will respond to the changes the princesses are bringing about."

"…Hearing you say that makes me glad to be your fiancé, Halphys," Marion replied with a kindhearted smile—one that I could finally accept as authentic and natural.

We could walk together, sharing the same thoughts and ideas. Knowing that gave me strength—and added further weight to my urge to spend my life with him.

"Thanks to her Thought Board, the Ministry of the Arcane is reevaluating Princess Anisphia and her magicology, too. The winds of change have certainly started to blow."

"I agree. I also think her theory of magicology can be applied to regular magic, too."

"I've heard that you've been busy putting something together lately… Is *that* what you're talking about?"

"Yes. I've been thinking about the incantations used to activate magical tools. By comparing them to the basic incantations used in conventional magic, I think we can devise a system that interprets magic differently from the current prevailing model. So I've been hard at work with my research…"

"That does sound interesting. Could you elaborate, Halphys?"

"If you wish, then certainly."

Marion was showing a legitimate interest in my recent studies, and now we had the opportunity to get into a lively debate, sharing our thoughts and opinions with each other.

If I had never met Princess Anisphia, I would probably still be casting my eyes to the ground. But that day, she paved the way for me to reach for the sky.

My first steps were probably rather small compared to those that others had taken, but even so, I was being driven by a strong urge to keep moving forward.

And so I held my head up high. This was no time to keep looking down. The way forward was open to me now.

* * *

The sun had already set, and night had fallen.

At this hour, most employees at the Ministry of the Arcane had already gone home. Yet I—Lang Voltaire—was still putting in overtime, pausing only to rub my tired eyes.

"Good work there, Lang," came a voice.

"…Is that you, Miguel?"

I glanced up and saw that Miguel had indeed entered my office without so much as knocking. His cheerful and flippant tone was truly loathsome.

Despite his ill manners, he was still the son of a marquis—which only added to my consternation.

"It's fine to burn the midnight oil, but don't push yourself too hard, eh?" he told me. "If you aren't careful, it won't just be your shoulders that go stiff—your heart will freeze up, too."

"Your concern is noted. You do like to make pointless conversation, don't you?"

"What an awful thing to say. And here I am worried about you." Miguel cackled as he folded his hands behind his head.

I hated these little quirks of his. He didn't know how to show the slightest semblance of respect.

"You always put work first, so I thought I had no choice but to come and check it out for myself," he said, reaching out to touch the Thought Board that I was using to type up a document.

I wrinkled my brow in annoyance.

The Thought Board was a magical tool, one created by Princess Anisphia and brought here by Princess Euphyllia. I had to admit that it was extremely useful, although it was very annoying to have this pointed out to me, especially by Miguel.

"...I'm not prejudiced against magical tools in and of themselves."

"It's pretty much the same thing, though, don't you think? You still don't like Princess Anisphia, am I right?"

"...Not that I could just go and admit that," he muttered. He sounded surprisingly bitter, even to me.

No, I couldn't accept Princess Anisphia or her innovative and heretical ideas, and I despised her disrespect to the very existence of spirits.

Nonetheless, she had produced tangible accomplishments. And this time was no exception. Her ideas and creations did have value—value so great that they could end up changing the world.

When someone or something was recognized for their value, it was natural for others to flock around them. They could sense the tides turning.

…And that was why, ever since I'd realized this possibility, I had to keep driving these preparations.

"Don't push yourself too hard," Miguel said.

"…Why does it give me the chills, hearing you offer up encouragement?"

"Wow, no mercy from you. I'm helping you here. It's only natural to be concerned, eh?"

"And I *am* grateful… I don't know if it's too early or too late for me to make a move now. But I owe you for your help."

"That's what I call a conflict of interest. We want to get the Ministry of the Arcane fixed up as soon as possible. When it comes down to it, we're just the behind-the-scenes guys. But I would like to step out into the open for once," Miguel said with a fearless grin.

Beneath his frivolous attitude lurked something akin to a sharp blade. I could feel it pressing up against my throat as I broke out into a cold sweat.

Is he really the son of a marquisal family, one that provided several directors for the Ministry of the Arcane and established itself in the shadows as a neutral voice…? I'm really starting to dislike him.

Indeed, this flippant man excelled at provoking me. His usual demeanor was probably a front intended to hide his true talent. I understood full well what he was doing, but I still didn't like it.

…And I wasn't particularly happy that I needed to rely on help from the likes of him.

"…Those in positions of authority must fulfill their responsibilities," I said. "That's all there is to it. So I, too, must carry out my duties."

"You're very earnest."

"Most people are, at least compared to you."

"You're not wrong there!"

I briskly slapped away Miguel's hand as he clapped me on the shoulder. Damn him, but he could be depressing.

"Seriously, though, I'm worried about you. If you make one wrong move, you'll end up getting hurt."

"…Hmph. I'm aware of that."

"You don't fully approve of Princess Anisphia yet, do you? What are your thoughts there? Let me know what you honestly think. Besides, I'm about the only person actually listening to you right now."

True, still he maintained that frivolous attitude, but his eyes seemed to peer deep into my soul. There was no reason why I ought to respond to such a look, but regardless, I began letting my feelings slip from pure exhaustion.

"…I don't know, so I'm trying not to think about it. Right now, I'm pursuing the ministry's best interests. My personal feelings and beliefs can take a back seat. Otherwise, the ministry's prestige will fall even further, into bedrock territory. And it might not end with the ministry, either. The changes these people will bring about will be irreversible."

"Irreversible, huh? Once you know, you can't go back, eh? That's certainly true. I've learned that life with magical tools is completely different from life without them."

"…It's terrifying. What awaits us in a world where everything has changed? Will there be a place for me there? Will there be anything left for me to believe in?"

I leaned back in my chair and covered my eyes. As my vision darkened, my worries began to take tangible shape. So this was fear. Intimidated by the prospect of change, my heart was gripped by the anxiety of advancing headfirst into an uncertain future.

"…You joined the Ministry of the Arcane after graduating from the academy, right?" Miguel asked.

"…Why are you asking something so obvious? Of course I did."

"Did your parents ever bring you here while you were a kid?"

"No. I don't know about other families, by my father was very strict on that point. He would say to me that if you want to enter through these gates, you have to prove your worthiness through your own efforts."

"You Voltaires are an uptight bunch, huh? Is that why you're always so serious?" Miguel cackled.

I fixed him with a glare, prompting him to shrug and raise his hands in surrender.

"Right then. So I guess you never met her?" he asked. "That was long before you joined the ministry, after all…"

"What are you talking about?"

"Long, long ago, there used to be a girl who would excitedly come and go through the Ministry of the Arcane."

I felt my eyebrows climbing up my forehead. What on earth was Miguel saying? I had a hunch, but I couldn't be entirely sure.

"She was already famous even back then. Whenever she showed up at the ministry, she would have a twinkle in her eye. She was tiny, just a little girl, but she kept insisting how she wanted to learn magic."

"…That's—"

"But as much as she longed for magic, she simply wasn't able to wield it."

I fell silent after this interruption. Who in the world was he talking about? But the reason I couldn't say anything in response was because I already knew the answer.

"The girl wasn't stupid. In fact, she was remarkably bright for her age. At first, everyone thought that, with her smarts, she *must* have a latent talent for magic. But it just wouldn't work for her. She had no ability at all, not a speck of it, strangely enough."

"…"

"Everyone thought there had to be some kind of mistake, so they kept trying to teach her to use magic for herself. They gave her all kinds of lessons, instructed her on the nature of spirits and how to properly revere them. The girl was desperate, willing to try anything and everything."

But in the end, none of it worked.

"Expectation turned to disappointment. Everyone here pitied her. It's ironic, don't you think?" Miguel asked nonchalantly, though his expression was now inscrutable.

I knew about this girl, too, although many aspects of her past remained unknown to me. Now I was being confronted with those raw details.

"I guess she just couldn't give up," Miguel continued. "She read so many books that she seemed ready to break, and she prayed ardently. But it wasn't enough to change anything. She simply didn't have the gift of magic. And that was an absolute fact. If it had ended there with her tears, this story would have been a tragedy."

…Except she didn't end up becoming a tragic heroine.

I knew full well what followed—and I could hardly stand it.

The girl began investigating magic on her own, espousing theories that everyone found utterly outlandish. Some of them were even sacrilegious to tradition and faith.

In time, people's sympathy turned to disgust. But the girl didn't stop ploughing forward, even after society had begun to shun her, until—

"I didn't actually see her, either. I only heard about it all secondhand," Miguel murmured.

He was simply stating the facts, calmly, plainly. And they were the sins that we had all accumulated.

"After a while, no one listened to the girl's ideas anymore. They say she wept, that she kept on appealing to everyone. Insisting that she wouldn't give up, so would someone, anyone, please listen to her? But no one did. They considered her a waste of time, her suggestions nothing more than a child's fantasies. And so, for a while, she stopped appealing to us all. She paid no attention to those who had denied her. She began to act up, and her selfishness gave rise to delinquency."

"…What's the point of all this?"

"Of what?"

"What are you trying to accomplish telling me these things?"

"You mean about this girl who had no hope for or trust in the future, but who's now making strides? How scared do you think *she* was? How anxious? Well, Lang?"

Miguel's voice was devoid of emotion, his eyes fixed on me as though sizing me up. What did he find? Was I good or evil? Right or wrong?

"If that girl could succeed where you can't, I guess it must have been her who was right, wouldn't you say?"

...Those fatal words pierced deep into my heart.

If I could, I would have vomited blood. But I held back, gritting my teeth and clenching my fists to keep the bile from rising up inside me.

"Well, I'm not on either side, though," Miguel added.

"...What?"

"I mean, both sides are wrong, you know? You're both right, too, but you're also equally wrong. The girl gave up on everyone too soon to produce concrete results, and the ministry was too quick to give up on her, and then they refused to listen to her afterward. It's like both sides kept on throwing stones at the other without ever compromising to meet halfway. It's pretty stark and barren, I guess."

"...Stark? Barren?" I murmured, but those words held no power.

Closing my eyes, I could see the girl flashing a carefree smile that I couldn't bring myself to like.

"I know you're working hard, Lang. You're too serious and inflexible, and you don't know how to relax. I don't think what you're doing is wrong, per se. But then again, you can't claim that everyone who thinks differently than you is wrong, either, yes?"

"...Yeah, I suppose not."

"It's fine to dig around and lay the groundwork behind the scenes. There aren't many who can do that. But it's pretty stupid to refuse to compromise, to never set foot from the box you've drawn yourself into. There's nothing wrong with an emotionless pursuit of results, but people don't live to carry out a role, you realize?"

"...I believe that the way forward will reveal itself only after I've fulfilled my role."

"Then why don't you go and talk to someone who's already done it and knows what's on the other side?"

Realizing what Miguel meant by that, I slowly opened my eyes. He was smiling—his usual impenetrable smile.

"I don't think it's a bad bet, if I do say so myself. After all, she's still madly in love with the idea of magic."

CHAPTER 6
Exchanging Words, Discussing the Future

It was a holiday, yet the villa at the detached palace was filled with quiet tension.

An unusually large number of faces had gathered in the parlor—me, Euphie, Ilia, Lainie, Halphys, and Garkie.

And sitting across from us were Lang, Marion, and Miguel—the three of them having come from the Ministry of the Arcane.

I could find no words to describe the atmosphere, which was broken only when Lang spoke up first. "Thank you very much for taking the time to see us today."

"I was a little surprised to hear that you wanted to pay us a visit, Lang," I replied.

Yes, the reason for this meeting was that he had approached me. Ever since hearing that he wanted to talk, I couldn't help but wonder what exactly was going on.

He had offered to accompany Marion and Miguel, and had let me know that Halphys and Garkie could sit in, too, if I thought it necessary.

I had no idea what the point of discussion would be, but I'd asked them both to join us if they wanted.

"Now, there's no need to be diplomatic or offer lip service," I said. "Would you mind cutting to the chase?"

"Very well. Then allow me to speak plainly. Princess Anisphia, Princess Euphyllia—what do you wish to do with the Ministry of the Arcane?" Lang asked.

"...As I've told you before, I just think it would be nice if we could all get along," I answered.

"Then what about you, Princess Euphyllia?"

"I want to overhaul the ministry," she replied. "Looking ahead, I believe it will need long-term reforms."

"But does that goal not deny the role of the Ministry of the Arcane? You talk about compromise, but to what extent do you think compromise necessary?"

"...Let me ask *you* a question—what exactly is your concern, Lang?" Euphie asked.

Lang pursed his lips and closed his eyes. Then, after a long pause, he said: "What I fear...is the dissolution of the ministry, Princess Euphyllia."

Euphie was visibly shocked. For my part, I had never once considered dismantling the Ministry of the Arcane—but for Lang to bring it up like this, he must have considered that prospect likely.

"If Princess Anisphia promotes the spread of magicology and these magical tools, that would be in conflict with the ministry," he continued. "For that reason, I understand your goals of encouraging reform, Princess Euphyllia. However, I would like to know what you envision after having accomplished these reforms. If they lead to the demise of the ministry, I feel compelled to offer my own opinions."

"Do you really think we can destroy the Ministry of the Arcane on our own?"

"Not at present. But it would be possible once Your Highness accedes to the throne."

"...I suppose it could be. But there wouldn't be any need for that, would there?"

"Why not?"

"Why not...? The Ministry of the Arcane is the largest organization in the whole Kingdom of Palettia."

"It isn't a question of size, but whether Your Highness and your associates believe it should continue to exist," Lang said with a shake of his head, his quiet words carrying strong weight. "Now that the truth behind spirit covenants has come to light, there is no end to the number of individuals questioning our beliefs in spirits themselves. Whether we like it or not, we are entering a period of change. However, we have served the Kingdom of Palettia for generations to preserve our traditions and faith. Change isn't something that we can accept so easily—not right away."

"I understand that," I told him. "Or rather, I'm trying to understand. Which is why I've never considered abolishing the Ministry of the Arcane. Even if I or Euphie was to be the kingdom's next ruler."

"That's right," Euphie added. "The Ministry of the Arcane is irreplaceable."

The ministry served the kingdom as a political advisory body, facilitated public events, and stored and understood a wide range of documentation that they used to conduct historical research and study magical techniques. Each of these functions was indispensable to the realm.

"I'm not considering driving the ministry out of the political arena," I explained, "and with the experience and knowledge it's accumulated over the years, it's the best facilitator of events and functions. So dismantling it would be out of the question."

"It will be necessary to continue magic research into the future," Euphie added. "Even if the use of magical tools becomes widespread, there will still be a need for magic. I hope that wider understanding of Anis's magicology will lead to a breakthrough in new magic research."

"That's right," I continued. "It's true I've had problems with the ministry, and maybe I don't exactly feel like getting along with people who have always spurned me, but that doesn't mean I'll treat you all unfairly. If possible, I'd like to come to a compromise. I mean it, honestly."

"...A compromise? Is that really your true intention, Princess Anisphia?" Lang asked.

"I'm being sincere here. I'm pretty sure I've said this before, but I've been reflecting on some of my mistakes, too. True, there are a lot of things I can't forgive, but I don't think that eliminates the need for the ministry."

"In that case, Princess Euphyllia, you are convinced that Princess Anisphia's magical tools and her magicology will reshape the kingdom. But you are interested not in aligning yourself with her, but in embarking on this project of reforming the Ministry of the Arcane. What exactly are *your* intentions?" Lang asked, shifting his attention.

Euphie remained unwavering as she answered him. "The reason I'm doing this is to connect the traditions of the past to the future that Anis will forge from here on out. Anis's future is filled with possibilities, but within those many potential outcomes, there are some that will allow us to maintain a connection with our past. Yet there remains a great gulf between past and future. I believe it's my mission to help bridge that divide."

"You're saying that our inherited traditions and Princess Anisphia's envisioned future are at a disconnect? Do you really think it possible to join the two?" Lang pressed.

"If we don't, one of them will end up being abandoned. I don't want that to happen, which is why I've taken the position that I have."

Lang fell silent at this response. Neither Marion nor Miguel had spoken yet; the former was visibly nervous, and the latter, strangely enough, was nonchalantly requesting a second cup of tea. I found his attitude more than a little frustrating.

"...I cannot agree with Princess Anisphia's ideology. I can't help but feel a sense of reluctance when faced with it. The day may never come when I think that your magicology, which disparages existing teachings and the very existence of spirits, is correct." Lang let out an agonized sigh as he shook his head.

"...That can't be helped, then," I said. "If that's the way things are, there's nothing I can do about it."

"Yes. But you would never have admitted that in the past. You changed your behavior and showed us by your actions that you are willing to compromise. That being the case, I suppose it's now our turn."

"...Lang?"

"I believe that reform of the Ministry of the Arcane and its consequent downsizing is inevitable. Still, I would like to ask you to do as much as you can to accommodate those who have served the realm. If you will pledge that guarantee, I offer you my loyalty, Your Highnesses," he said, bowing deeply.

I noticed his bunched fists trembling on his knees.

"…If we change the way the ministry works, there will inevitably be times when we will have to ask those not in line with future plans to step down," Euphie said. "But I understand what you're asking. I promise to help as many people as I can find their way."

"I'd prefer if we didn't have to dismiss anyone," I added. "I've got a complicated history with the ministry, but I don't want to see the institution gone."

"Yep, yep. So it's settled then? I bet you're relieved, aren't you, Lang?" Miguel said, as though intentionally misreading the room.

Lang let out a tired sigh. The tension began to dissipate.

"This isn't the ministry's full consensus or anything," Miguel continued, "but Lang here was preparing to persuade people to cooperate with you, Your Highnesses."

"Is that so?" I asked.

"Well, if things keep going the way they are, you'll both have to shoulder the ministry's personnel issues, too, right? And public opinion is leaning in your favor. If we don't come up with any solutions soon, we'll be pushed into a corner. But if they think they're at risk of losing their positions, it's only natural that some people won't want to go along with it all."

"I'm aware."

"Lang has been laying the groundwork looking for those who might be able to be brought around. Heck, I was the one getting all the information for him. I was thinking of asking Your Highnesses to make good use of it as a bargaining chip…but I hear you've got pretty decent eyes and ears of your own, too. You've even recruited someone I've had my own eye on. Isn't that right, missy?" Miguel said, turning to Lainie with a smile.

As she drew back in alarm, Ilia stepped forward, fixing Miguel with a menacing glare. But he remained as aloof as ever. Marion rubbed his eyebrows with apparent exhaustion.

"Please stop all this impropriety, Miguel," he said. "Besides, from what I heard, it wasn't a major development."

"I asked Marion to assist Princess Euphyllia because it was still in the early stages. I suppose you can think of it like an additional benefit."

"I won't deny that, but even so—"

"Forgive me, Marion, but I've only recently been able to formulate my current thoughts," said Lang. "I had to gauge the princesses' true intentions before I could make my decision."

"You're too cautious, Lang. You've prepared for either outcome no matter how this conversation goes."

"...I'm glad we didn't end up fighting one another, Lang," Euphie said.

"I haven't decided *not* to fight you yet," he told her. "If I find that the path you're setting out on will prove detrimental to the kingdom, then I will change my position."

"Yes, I understand. I hope we can build a positive relationship from here on out."

"...In that case, I have a proposal to make to Your Highnesses."

"A proposal?"

"Two, actually. First, I would like you, Princess Euphyllia, to take charge at the Ministry of the Arcane. I know you've been working on solidifying your base, but that has only been on the level of individual associates. You haven't yet been recognized as leading a faction of your own. So I would like to take this opportunity to let it be known that a new faction has been formed, led by you, Lady Euphyllia."

"...Yes," she replied. "You're right. What I have can't quite be called a faction as of yet. If you're willing to provide your cooperation, I would be most grateful."

"In the future, let's host an evening party or a banquet to spread the word. I believe it would be ideal if we could persuade those powerbrokers who aren't keen on cooperating with your agenda to step down as well."

"...Do you think so? Some might consider that a betrayal if they found out, no?" Euphie asked with a suspicious frown.

Lang, however, shook his head. "At present, they can still choose to retire with honor. Those who can't see which way the wind is blowing are not qualified to hold positions of power and responsibility. Knowing when to step aside is a necessary skill."

"...I see," she responded with some difficulty.

I understood perfectly well how she must have felt. After all, I didn't want to crush those who opposed me. I didn't want to leave behind any sparks that could one day cause a violent conflagration.

Nonetheless, some conflicts simply couldn't be avoided, and it wouldn't be possible to save everyone. Some at the ministry were like Lang, but not all. We would have to decide whom we could save and whom we couldn't. Bearing that responsibility was what it meant to stand at the top.

I guess I really am unsuited to ruling as queen. I hate having to choose. I always end up wanting to run away from decisions like this...

I couldn't help heaving a tired sigh upon being reminded that I wasn't suited to the role. But I couldn't let myself get depressed again, and so I pulled myself back together.

"So your first proposal is to advertise that a new faction has formed around Euphie, right?" I asked. "And your second suggestion?"

"It's related to the first one, but I would like to lean on your wisdom here, Princess Anisphia."

"My wisdom...?"

"I would like your help to bring in those at the ministry who remain neutral. It would be ideal if the Ministry of the Arcane and Your Highness could jointly accomplish something to that end."

I gaped, speechless with surprise. I couldn't help but look him over, hoping to gauge his true intentions.

"As I believe I touched on earlier, in my view, a reduction in the size of the ministry is inevitable. The reason for this is that as magicology becomes more widespread, there will be those who elect to pursue a career in that field of study. As such, I am concerned that reverse discrimination may occur between traditional researchers and those interested in magicology."

"...Reverse discrimination? You're suggesting that traditional research may be neglected by a turn to magicology?"

"Yes. I see that future as unavoidable."

"You've been thinking far ahead... I suppose it isn't impossible."

"...Are you that worried?" Euphie asked, frowning in disbelief at Lang's negative outlook. "I don't think magical tools can replace traditional magic just yet..."

"Not yet maybe," I said. "But one day perhaps, Euphie. And that isn't good."

"It isn't?"

"Lang is concerned because he's thinking even further into the future. Isn't that right?" I turned back to Lang.

"...I wouldn't have expected you to notice that," he replied, drawing in his shoulders as he breathed a sigh.

Euphie was still tilting her head to one side, as if she didn't quite grasp the predicament.

Instead, Halphys spoke up. "You're referring to a decline in spiritualist faith?"

Those words prompted everyone to fall silent.

After a long moment, Lang nodded in reply. "Yes. That's my concern. If magical tools become more widespread and people are more capable of defending themselves, the role of the nobility will diminish. That would, in turn, lead to a loss of opportunities to see the tangible benefits of magic and, at the same time, a decline in our faith."

"...You're exaggerating a little there, aren't you?" Garkie murmured weakly.

"I may be overreacting, but it remains a possibility that we cannot afford to ignore."

This time, Garkie had no response.

"Wait a minute," Euphie cut in, unable to accept what she was hearing. "It's true that the use of traditional magic may decrease somewhat, but magical tools are designed to imitate magic, and they still draw on the power of spirits. I don't think belief in spirits in and of itself would come to an end..."

I understood what she was trying to say there—but at the same time, I couldn't claim that Lang's concerns were groundless, either.

"...Maybe it would be more accurate to say that the backbone of people's faith would be replaced with something else?" I suggested.

"Replaced...?"

"People's faith in magic up till now could be redirected to magical tools. If we're not careful, it could lead to the disappearance of spiritualist culture itself."

Should magical tools be widely adopted, the essential aspects of that faith—gratitude for and belief in spirits—would remain the same. However, there could be little doubt that it would entail a radical transformation away from conventional spirit worship.

"It's just a possibility, but if magical tools become mainstream, maybe one day in the future, mages might become the heretics. After all, there would be far more people who can't use magic."

"...They could be treated as heretics simply because they're mages...?"

"Mages are accepted in the Kingdom of Palettia because they fulfill various duties as nobles," I explained. "But what if we no longer needed nobles to fulfill those duties? Or if people decided they didn't want nobles? Changing the backbone of the faith could lead to the possibility of persecution."

"...Oh." Euphie's eyes widened as it all dawned on her.

As a general rule, people feared and rejected heresy. That was unavoidable. So what might lie on the other side once the public lost their reverence for mages? Envy and fear of those who possess powers that they do not.

Now, nobles were respected *because* they could wield magic. But mages outside the nobility were regarded as individuals possessed of fiendish powers.

In fact, there had at times been incidents involving mage bandits— obviously not nobles—inflicting grave damage. There was no telling when an entity capable of overwhelming power might turn on society. Personally, I agreed that it would be impossible to permit such beings to remain at one's side.

"Lang is certainly overstating the predicament," I said. "But we can't say that the future he's worried about is impossible, either. Even now, the nobility and the common folk aren't exactly on good terms."

"...If such a future should come to pass, I would feel empty inside." Lang's expression was tinged with sorrow.

It would have been easy to laugh at his worries or dismiss them out of hand—but I knew that I, too, would feel restless if I were in his position.

"If we're destined for a future in which mages are superfluous, then what will become of the nobility? Would our pride be nothing more than an errant mistake lost in the flow of time? In that case, then why did we ever exist?" His face downcast, he clasped his hands together above his forehead as though in prayer—his words sounding like a cry of repentance.

Just how much was he suffering? I couldn't help but feel a sense of déjà vu as I watched. I knew the pain of despairing when you knew that what you wanted to believe in simply would never come to pass.

The end of the nobility's role in society. Ultimately, it might be a surprisingly simple affair. Magical tools would become widespread, and people would be able to confront monsters themselves without the protection of the aristocracy.

Would those nobles, having been rendered unnecessary, lose all value? Would there be any point to continuing as a noble? My ideals could end up undermining their whole sense of worth.

But even so, I had a different view on it all.

"Lang, I've always been fascinated by magic. That was the beginning of all of this. For me, being a mage was an ideal I was always chasing after. I don't hate you all. I just wanted to be like you."

*   *   *

But I couldn't. I had no innate talent for magic. I couldn't reach the ideal that I so desperately wanted, and no matter how hard I searched for any possible path, none was open to me.

"But I couldn't give up, so I turned to magicology. It was the only form of magic that I could use. And I didn't create it to deny past forms of magic. I just…I just wanted to dream the same dreams as the rest of you."

I longed for magic, and I wanted to fulfill my duties as a mage, to be the person I ought to be.

In this country where magic is absolute, there will inevitably be born people who aren't capable of wielding it. People who suffer as I had.

But magic, as it existed now, wasn't everything. I prayed that magic could offer many, many more possibilities.

Far from being accepted, I was criticized, undermined—and at some point, I stopped seeking others' sympathy. Yet I wanted magic to be filled with hopes and dreams, like stars glimmering in the night sky. Like finding even the smallest of lights up above.

"I've created something that could cause the nobility to lose the thing that defines them as nobles. I can't deny that, but I don't exactly see it the same way. I couldn't stand to have my dreams taken away just because of some innate talent. So what does anyone's status matter if they want to dream?"

"…You're saying status is irrelevant when it comes to dreams?" Lang asked.

"I might end up killing the aristocracy's role. But being a noble is still an ideal I dream about. The nobility won't disappear—no, I don't *want* it to disappear. It's the pride of the kingdom, isn't it? Even if that role changes, I don't think everyone will abandon the wishes entrusted to the nobles. The powerful protect the powerless, and their honor and pride all come from the fact that they *are* powerful. But I want to live in a world where *everyone* can feel a sense of pride—not just because they're nobles."

Lang glanced up, staring across at me as though trying to read my thoughts. I responded with a confident smile, all but declaring that I had nothing to be ashamed of.

"Are we truly moving in opposing directions, Lang? We might not share the same opinions or ideologies, but I find it hard to believe we're looking at entirely different goals."

"...Princess Anisphia."

"I want a world where everyone can be different and where everyone can think that those differences are wonderful. So let's find that future together. A place where mages, even if no longer nobles, can continue to exist among the people."

Hearing my declaration, Lang let out a quiet exhale. His gaze remained downcast for a moment, but when he finally looked up, I found a sense of calm in his demeanor for the first time.

"Someone once described you as the princess who most adored magic, but whom magic didn't love back."

"...I've heard people say that."

"Whether magic loves you or not, it's no exaggeration to say that your love for magic is true. I feel like I can honestly acknowledge that now."

"...I never thought the day would come when I'd hear those words coming out of your mouth. Life's a strange thing, isn't it?"

Profound expressions fell over both our faces as we reconciled.

The atmosphere that now filled the room was beyond description. I requested a fresh pot of tea so that we could all start over. Once that was ready, everyone returned to their seats.

"So in summary: What you're asking for, Lang, is a reconciliation between me and the Ministry of the Arcane, and you want to establish a new position for mages once the spread of magical tools begins to affect spirit worship. Is that correct?"

"Yes. I do think that future is a long way off, but we cannot afford to wait. If we can begin preparations now, I would very much like to do so."

"Hmm…" I let out a low moan, placing my elbows on my knees as I rested my chin in my hands.

Yep, Lang's requests wouldn't be easy to fulfill.

If I had to guess, his fears wouldn't come to pass for a few decades, if ever. Even if nobles were no longer sought after for their magic abilities, they were still highly educated. Politics, for instance, was the exclusive realm of the aristocracy.

But that didn't mean they weren't replaceable. The spread of magical tools would bring great benefits to the common people, and as their lives improved—as they became more affluent and resourceful—they would have increased opportunities to pursue an education. It wouldn't be surprising to one day find bureaucratic aristocrats rising from the ranks of commoners.

If that happened, the prestige that came with being a noble would inevitably diminish. In the end, there might even come a future when mages were no longer needed by anyone and were persecuted as heretics for possessing arcane powers.

"So if we're to avoid a future like that, we'll need to change the very nature of the nobility," I said in summary.

"As the realm evolves, so, too, must those who administer it. But we need more than vague notions about change and adaptation—we need concrete guidance."

"…Ultimately, I think the root of the problem is the huge divide and disconnect between the nobility and the common people."

If mages were persecuted in the future, the cause would be others' fear and jealousy toward them. Given that mages were currently responsible for defending the people from monsters and the like, they were presently safe from persecution.

But if that premise was lost, the future that Lang feared would be more likely to come to pass. Indeed, it would be ideal if the aristocratic class had a positive relationship with the masses before such a time came around.

"The problem is all the corruption in the nobility, isn't it? It's impossible to build closer bonds when the people feel downtrodden…"

"You mean resolving the disputes that exist between commoners and the nobility? It's certainly regrettable that the number of inadequate nobles has increased in recent years…but if armed with magical tools, the people won't need nobles at all. That could result in the two groups growing even more distant."

"Right—if commoners were equipped to defend themselves, they would no longer need mages to serve as a defensive force. So basically, it would be best if they could serve a different role, something other than offering protection, to earn the respect of the common folk that way…"

"Besides offering protection, you say…?"

"Hmm… There's always a demand for healing magic and the like… Maybe we could set up a system to make it easier to receive medical treatment than exists now?" I suggested.

"That's a promising idea, but it will only benefit those who actually can use healing magic. I feel that we'll need to increase the value of the nobility more broadly," Lang countered.

"More broadly? To reaffirm the value of the nobility itself…?"

I frowned and *hmm*ed. It wasn't easy coming up with concrete ideas on the spot.

"It's magic that the nobility has and that commoners don't, right?" I said. "So it would be best if the Ministry of the Arcane could take the lead in activities that increase the perceived value of nobles *as* mages."

"In other words, even if magical tools become commonplace, we could demonstrate that they aren't a substitute for some of the benefits of magic?" Euphie placed her hand over her mouth as she sank deep in thought.

"Something that's impossible with magical tools, that only traditional magic can accomplish… There aren't many magical tools at present, so in that regard, there are a lot of things that haven't been replaced yet," I offered. "Then again, if we took the time to develop more, we might be able to surpass traditional magic in terms of the variety of uses and the like."

"…So you're saying that the mages' days are numbered?" Garkie muttered softly.

The entire room fell silent at these words. Mages were nobles, and as nobles, their raison d'être was to protect the realm and to enrich the people's lives.

The Kingdom of Palettia couldn't have been founded without the power of magic, but now that magical tools had been created to replace traditional magic, it was obvious that the era in which mages reigned supreme would one day reach an end. After all, magical tools could be used by anyone and could be produced in large number.

Moreover, precisely because they were tools, they were inherently stabler, whereas the efficacy of traditional magic depended on the skill of individual mages.

"Something that only a mage can do...? Like a spirit covenant?"

"That's out of the question," Euphie said, aghast.

She was busy trying to change public awareness of spirit covenants, so setting that as our goal would be to put the cart before the horse.

"...No, hold on. Spirits..." All of a sudden, Euphie grew pensive; it was like a lightbulb had switched on in her head.

Had she realized something important?

"...Lang," she began. "It's only a possibility, but I might have an idea that could straighten everything out."

"Really?" Lang asked, staring back at her with confusion.

Marion likewise looked conflicted, while Miguel let out a gleeful whistle before adding, "Heh, so Princess Euphyllia has a plan. I wonder what in the world she's come up with?"

"I can't say for sure if it will work just yet, so can I ask you all to drop by again once I've had a chance to look into it?" she suggested.

No one had any objections, so Lang, Marion, and Miguel's visit came to an end, for us to reconvene at a later date.

* * *

That evening, Euphie and I were drinking some after-dinner tea and taking a bath.

"So what's this idea you came up with, Euphie?" I asked.

"When everyone started talking about spirit covenants, well, it reminded me of something. It's about Lumi…"

"Lumi? What about her?"

The spirit covenantor Lumi, full name Lumielle René Palettia—our ancestor and the daughter of the first king. She visited the detached palace every now and then seemingly on a whim, sharing tea and teasing my father and Duke Grantz while they were working.

She didn't show herself to others, though. In a way, she was like a phantom or specter, appearing and disappearing seemingly at will. But what could she have to do with all this?

"When I met Lumi, I saw a materialized spirit," Euphie said.

"A materialized spirit…?" I repeated.

"Yes. It looked like a miniature person, and it had wings."

"Oh? Seriously? You're sure it was a spirit?"

"I'm sure. At the time, Lumi was singing a song—and song is just another kind of incantation. So I think it was magic…"

"You're spot on… I think that's the saying, no?"

Out of nowhere, a voice sounded out. Euphie and I were both taken by surprise, each of us visibly startled.

By the moonlit window sat a mysterious young girl—Lumi—eyeing us reproachfully.

"…Can't you make a better entrance? You know, in a way that doesn't give us both a heart attack?" I said.

"Oh? There's no task more uphill than preaching common sense to a spirit covenantor, you know."

"I'm aware of that! You are so insufferable!"

"I've heard the same said about you, Anis," Lumi teased with a grin.

"Ngh! Shut up! Shut up!"

I really didn't appreciate a retort like that coming from her.

"Good evening, Lumi," Euphie interjected. "Was my guess correct?"

"Indeed, Euphie. As you've inferred, spirits can be materialized through magic."

"Can only spirit covenanters use magic like that?"

"There is a certain condition necessary for a spirit to materialize, but it doesn't necessarily need a covenantor to fulfill it. Of course, being a spirit covenantor yourself, you should be able to understand it someday."

"What kind of condition?"

"The ability to use magic. That's all. The end result of wielding magic is the materialization of spirit, bestowing will, thought, and the ability to move independently. It's rather similar to the start of life. Just as the gods once brought spirits into the world and created all things."

"This has moved to an extraordinary scale..."

"Spirits are fragments of the world. To shape those fragments into your desired form, even a self-sustaining one, is to tap into the realm of the divine. Then again, it's only temporary."

"Is that why you were singing?"

"Yes. Songs are made up of the thoughts, prayers, and history that we've passed down through the generations," Lumi said, flashing Euphie and me a tender smile.

A little unnerved, I found myself looking away.

"Since covenantors have themselves become spirits, it's simply easier to make other spirits take the form that you want. But in theory, anyone can materialize a spirit so long as they can visualize its complete form."

"Isn't that the difficulty?"

"Of course... Then again, knowing you two, I'm sure you'll have no trouble pulling it off."

"...What do you mean?"

"Magic is an illusion built of layered thoughts and given wings by your imagination. Through words and belief, it can perform all kinds of miracles. And through those miracles, building on knowledge of the principles of the world, you forge an image of what a spirit ought to be." Lumi waved her fingers through the air like a conductor, her words almost singsong in quality as she continued, "It's not an illusion but the deconstruction of the occult based on a real image. By pouring illusion into a true image, I discovered a new form of magic. Two contradictory ways of being that coexist simultaneously. The only difference is the starting point and the process. The spirits and the world will never reject it. What I'm trying to say…is the paths overlap."

I felt as though Lumi's words had caught my heart within their grip.

I could hardly keep up with my own feelings as they washed over me. I was aware that I was in some kind of shock, yet at the same time, I was puzzled by my inability to recognize it for what it was.

But before I could fully ascertain this uncertain feeling, Lumi burst into laughter. "Ah, it never grows old. I'm going to live for a long, long time. Well then, I guess we're done here, so I'll let you two youngsters get some rest."

"You don't need to put it like that! We can look after ourselves!" I blurted out in frustration.

But all it took was a blink of the eye and Lumi had disappeared, vanished into the wind.

"Argh! She's so selfish and impulsive! Doesn't she ever stop and think about how much she bothers people?!"

"…Anis, do you need a mirror?"

"What's *that* supposed to mean, Euphie?"

"Well…" She giggled, staring back at me.

Pursing my lips, I turned away from her.

"But she's given me a hint—almost an answer, in fact," Euphie added.

"…Don't tell me you're going to get the Ministry of the Arcane to materialize spirits."

"It would be impossible for a magical tool to do that, don't you think? Even if they can handle the power of spirits, it would take too much time and effort to materialize a spirit itself to get it to do something."

"…It's difficult enough even with artificial magicite. Right—I suppose materializing spirits would be beyond the realm of magical tools. That's only a meaningful goal for a mage."

The artificial magicite incorporated into the dresses that we used during the unveiling of our flying magical tools was designed to activate a specific kind of magic.

In the long term, we might be able to make an artificial spirit appear, but when it came to actually directing it, the technology would need to advance several steps further before we could actually do so.

And was it really necessary to go that far? At least for the time being, I wanted to focus on other magical tools that would be more in the kingdom's interest.

"But mages are a different matter. If they're no longer needed to serve as a defensive fighting force, it will be necessary to change a way of life that's deeply rooted in society. But it will be difficult to expect everyone to make use of magic for the benefit of the people."

"Yeah...I understand that, but what does that have to do with materializing spirits?" I asked, head tilted to one side in consternation.

Euphie flashed me a mischievous smile like a child who'd just come up with a prank. "It doesn't need to be useful at first."

"...It doesn't?"

"Mages can do things that the common people can't. So long as it doesn't hurt them, if it makes them feel something, if it prompts their imaginations and helps them to connect, isn't that enough? So I think it would be ideal if the Ministry of the Arcane could hold an event and materialize spirits through song."

But she wasn't finished. As though unveiling her cherished dreams, she continued:

"It's wonderful to be able convey to future generations everything we've inherited through the ages. So wouldn't it be even more joyous if we could use the magic that we once used for fighting to instead bring healing and enjoyment to others?"

...I found myself breathing a sigh of admiration.

Magic itself began with a wish—with the first king of the Kingdom of Palettia entering into a spirit covenant to protect the smiles and defend the happiness of those he loved from hardship and trial.

That wish ended up going too far, becoming deformed in the process, but it was corrected by Lumi's own wish. Thus the chain of wishes was passed on to the next generation.

And that led all the way to the present. Here we were, having inherited those wishes for ourselves. And now *we* were trying to change the future.

After the founding of the Kingdom of Palettia, the era of relying exclusively on the king came to an end, and the number of nobles working hand in hand increased. Now the era of relying on those same nobles was reaching its end.

Progress in the Kingdom of Palettia had been forged through magic. Magic to protect the happiness of the people, continuously expanding its reach. If that magic could be used not only to protect, but in some more meaningful way…

"…I think it's a beautiful dream. It's the very magic I always yearned for."

I was overjoyed to hear that she had such a brilliant vision for the future.

Knowing that the both of us were now marching toward the same dream filled me with peace of mind. I wasn't alone.

"…Hey, Euphie? Can I hold your hand?" I asked.

"My hand…? Yes, please. It's late; why don't we lie down?" she suggested.

She rose to her feet, holding her hand out for me to grasp. I took it in my own, then stood up, and the two of us made our way to the bed.

We lay down side by side on the mattress, our hands interlinked. As I turned toward her, my eyes met hers. Something about it all struck me as somehow amusing, and we both giggled.

"Say, Euphie?"

"What is it, Anis?"

"I want to spread the word even more. Just like we did with that mid-air waltz, I want everyone to know just how wonderful magic can be."

"I know you can do it, Anis."

Yep. After everything that had happened, I could say this with pride: I *could* do it, because I had Euphie by my side.

"...What kind of scene would you produce if you could materialize spirits?" I asked.

"Something beautiful. Like what Lumi showed me."

"No fair. Maybe I should beg her to show me next time?"

"...No, please don't do that."

"...? Why not?"

Euphie tugged my hand, pulling me into her arms.

"Because I'm your number one," she said. "If you start thinking Lumi's magic is better than mine...I'll get jealous, you know?"

"...You're *really* possessive."

"Because I'm your number one," she repeated.

Euphie grinned as if to drive the point home, then brought her face close to mine for a kiss. Was she hoping to forestall any potential rebuttal?

But I wasn't about to object, so I let her kiss me however she pleased.

CHAPTER 7
Anisphia's Birthday Gala

Several days after our chat with Lumi, Euphie had the same members as last time reconvene at the detached palace.

"The materialization of spirits...through song?"

Lang was the first to express his surprise and bewilderment at her proposal. Most of those present looked astonished, while Miguel chuckled with amusement.

"Materializing spirits through song? How's that work? Sounds like something from a fairy tale," he commented.

"If we can do it, it will attract the attention of nobles and the common people alike," said Euphie. "It will also help to deepen their faith in spirits by giving them visible form."

"...Yes, I suppose giving spirits a physical presence might be able to rehabilitate the reputation of the nobility, but isn't this only possible for covenantors?" Lang asked.

"Lady Lumi tells me it's simply a matter of effort. I myself have only been a spirit covenantor for a short time, but I understand the basic principle behind it. So I'll be happy to pass it on one day."

Lang was at a loss for words at this reply, rubbing the space between his eyebrows as though wrestling with a headache.

"I understand your concern," Euphie continued. "But everyone dreams of materializing a spirit at least once in their life, no? I thought if we could not only sense the presence of the spirits close to us, but see them, too..."

"...I won't deny that."

"There's no precedent for this, so it's only natural to approach it through trial and error. Still, it's worth pursuing, I think. Currently, only spirit covenantors can materialize spirits through song. I'm sure I'll be able to do it myself one day, but for a non-covenantor to learn it all from scratch would take tremendous effort. But it's Anis here who has made such difficult challenges surmountable."

"...In other words, you suggest building a magical tool to help assist in the effort?" Halphys asked, looking up with a start.

Euphie nodded in satisfaction. "Songs are used as a form of incantation, allowing spirits to temporarily take on physical form. If we understand the procedure, even if we lack the ability to perform it ourselves, we can create tools to help carry it out."

"Aha," Miguel replied giddily with a snap of his fingers. "And that will prove to everyone that the Ministry of the Arcane and Princess Anisphia here have worked out their differences."

Euphie was right. Who *wouldn't* want to see one of these spirits at least once in their life?

And this would require me and the ministry to cooperate in a joint research project, which would demonstrate to all that we were both willing to let bygones be bygones.

If Euphie could be credited with bridging the gulf that had existed between us, she would earn her place as its representative, while the ministry's reputation would be improved, too, addressing Lang's concerns.

"But can you actually build such a tool...?" he asked with a grim expression.

The next moment, everyone's gazes turned to me.

"Hmm," I began. "According to my theories, spirits are susceptible to the will and intentions of those invoking them and readily change form in response. So if we make the way we imagine them more concrete, we might be able to strengthen our connection to them..."

"I suspect we should be able to materialize them following the exact steps Anis is describing," Euphie agreed.

"In the end, the important thing is to convey your mental image to the spirit... If you can do that, I think an amplifier, something like a wand, might do the trick."

"An amplifier? Like a magic wand...?" said Lang. "But even if the process is an extension of what we already know, we still don't have any idea how to actually sublimate the magic to materialize them." He sighed.

The rest of the room appeared to nod along in agreement.

"Hmm." I paused to think. "I don't think it ought to be all that difficult, though."

"...You don't?"

"The spirits are already there. We just need to ask them to show themselves. I don't know what it's like, but surely you can all feel their presence, right?"

"We can feel them, but that doesn't mean we can sense their intentions."

"The will of a spirit mirrors that of the person invoking it. All you have to do is pray and they should reveal themselves. That's all there is to it—no more, no less. I mean, think about it. The first spirit covenantor didn't really have *any* magic at first, did he? Magic didn't come into being until *after* he made his covenant with the spirits."

"...Ah."

Even Euphie mustn't have realized all this, as her eyes widened. For those who could wield magic as a matter of course, it was instinctive, almost like breathing—but all the way back in the beginning, there wasn't so much as a single mage.

"So spirit covenants must have come *before* magic. The materialization of spirits may be an extension of magic, but I think pulling it off requires us to look back to the past rather than forward to the future. That first covenant was fulfilled back at a time when no one knew anything about magic. So the spirits were certainly there. Basically, materializing them isn't a question of skill or proficiency, but rather a wish to see them take form."

"...I see," Lang responded with a groan—he, too, seemed to be reaching a realization.

Seeing this response, I added further, "I don't really know how to phrase this... But as spirits mirror the people around them, then you need to let them know your sincerest wishes..."

"Convey your wishes?"

"Yes. I'll usher in an end to the era of mage-nobles serving to defend the realm. Once magical tools become widespread, there won't be any need for nobles to carry that responsibility alone. And that means changing the way we all interact with spirits, which has been more or less the same since the first covenant. What I'm trying to tell you is this—we don't need that original covenant anymore. But at the same time, we won't forget what it means to live alongside spirits."

Lang lifted his face, staring across at me. And he wasn't the only one—the others were quietly listening as well.

"Even if the way we interact with spirits changes, that doesn't change how valuable they are to us. It's just the people who change. Besides, there are some things that simply must stay the same. The role of the nobility will have to be reconsidered, but the promises that we've made to the spirits won't—our responsibility to protect the people's joy and happiness. I want to tell the spirits that, how the very first wish will never change."

"...And that will make them manifest?"

"*I* would love to communicate with them—to thank them for being my strength all this time," I said, gently placing my hand on my chest as I unburdened my heartfelt feelings. "People's lives will change, but I don't want to change that very first wish. I want to keep walking alongside the spirits. That's why I want to draw on song, on prayer, on wishes. If we can convey these thoughts, maybe we'll be able to offer the spirits physical form?"

From the first king to Lumi, then from Lumi to my own father's generation—and now those wishes and prayers had been passed on to us. The Kingdom of Palettia's history was intertwined with magic. And what's more, the beginning of that magic was also the happiness of the people.

Spirits didn't have clear thoughts or intentions of their own, yet they continued to coexist alongside people. And being the constants that they were, people turned to them with prayer.

"No matter how much our way of life might change, we must never forget that original wish. The past led the way to the present, and the present leads the way into the future. We need to pass it all on so that it isn't lost to time," I said, clutching my chest.

I couldn't let this feeling go. I couldn't let it just disappear.

"I'd tell them that we're happy. That we're changing so we can be happy, but that we'll never forget to show our appreciation to them. I want them to know we'll still be together, we'll still have fun together, we'll still live side by side."

If I could convey that my wish was genuine, I was sure the spirits would reveal themselves to us.

They wouldn't be transformed by magic but rather would act as a reflection of our own prayers. That was what I wanted to believe.

"Wow...," Lang breathed. He glanced away, his mouth opening then closing as though he wanted to say something. Finally, he heaved a long sigh to catch his breath before saying, "I don't think I have any better suggestions at the moment... In that case, let's try to materialize spirits through song."

"Right. First things first: We need to make sure we have the right tools for the job, yes?" I asked.

"It will depend on the tool itself, but something that can be used at special events would be ideal."

"So something that can assist with songs to materialize spirits, and that wouldn't be out of place at an official event... Hmm, I wonder..."

The first thing that singing brought to mind was a *microphone*. Perhaps a magic wand could work as one?

"...Musical instruments..."

With that murmuration of mine, the whole room fell silent, their gazes turning to a single point—Halphys.

"...Wouldn't it be possible to make a musical instrument–type magical tool…?" she asked. "Each part would have a function similar to a magic wand. What do you think…?"

"…Ah, I see. There are usually orchestra performances at official events, so there should be plenty of opportunities to use something like that," Garkie said with a clap of his hands.

"A musical instrument? Now that you mention it, those Thought Boards are a lot like keyboard instruments, and plenty of nobles learn music as a matter of etiquette. The groundwork's all in place, so to speak," Miguel breathed, his smile broadening with genuine awe.

"So it's settled? What do you think, Lang?" I asked.

"…I think so. It's an interesting idea. It would have a deep connection to music and song, and if you could build a magical tool resembling an instrument already to the nobility's tastes and use it to materialize spirits, you might even be able to silence all those hardheaded old men."

"Lang, you said you were going to organize a gathering sometime soon?" Euphie asked. "If your faction grows large enough to start taking the initiative, would we be able to schedule an event to be held in the near future?"

"That also makes sense, Princess Euphyllia. But if we want to attract attention, restore the ministry's reputation, and make a big show of reconciliation, it will need to be a rather large event."

"Yes. So first we'll need to take control over the faction. I assume you'll be fine with us coordinating individual personnel later, yes?"

"I don't mind. In the meantime, I would like to request that Princess Anisphia set to producing a musical instrument–type magical tool. Would that work?"

"Got it! I'll go discuss it with the craftsmen!"

* * *

Having established our goals, we each set out to complete our respective tasks.

Euphie, with Lainie by her side, was busy recruiting people to join Lang's faction at the Ministry of the Arcane.

I, on the other hand, spent my days shuttling back and forth between the palace and the castle town with Halphys and Garkie.

When I approached the craftsmen with an outline of a prototype, they readily accepted the request.

"A musical instrument–type magical tool? What exactly are we supposed to make?"

"You want to use a magic wand as reference? Hey, someone go talk to the magic wand artisans! Tell 'em Princess Anisphia is making a new magical tool! Haul 'em here by the scruff of the neck if you have to!"

"But how can you turn a musical instrument into a magical tool? Do you just have to put spirit stones inside it?"

"That would depend on the type of instrument we're talking about. Something nobles might like... Maybe a violin?"

"We could decorate the body with spirit stones, but that wouldn't be all that interestin'..."

"What if we mixed spirit stones into the construction? We could make a spirit stone–based paint?"

"That's it! We might have to reconsider if it affects the sound, but let's give it a try!"

...And so on, the craftsmen all talking merrily among themselves without my needing to intervene.

Out of everyone, it was Halphys who took the most active role. Having some experience playing the violin herself, perhaps she found it easier to express her opinions, as she was eagerly conversing with the gathered craftsmen.

Then, no sooner had the flurry of ideas drawn to a close than they set about constructing a prototype.

At first, I stuck around to oversee the production process—but it wasn't long before Duke Grantz asked me to resume my lectures on magical tools to various groups of nobles.

As such, I decided to leave day-to-day workshop supervision to Halphys. I was a little worried about letting her handle it all herself, but Euphie also sent along Marion from the Ministry of the Arcane, so we now had the two of them working together.

Then, once all that hectic activity was behind us, I was summoned by my parents. I stopped by my father's office and found both him and my mother sitting before a Thought Board, glancing up at me in unison.

"So you're here, Anis," my father said.

"Greetings, Father, Mother. How do you like the Thought Board?"

"It's not bad. If not for Grantz, I could honestly describe it as good."

"...You don't need to look at me like that. That's not my fault."

My mother and father were glaring at me, but to be honest, Duke Grantz had been an insane workaholic from the very beginning. All I'd done was make him more efficient.

"Come, sit down. Actually, there's something we need to tell you."

"A message?"

"Mm. We've already agreed to our part, but I'll let our next caller explain."

"Who's coming?"

"Someone you know very well," my mother said. This sounded like the setup for a practical joke.

Huh? Who could it be? Just as I tilted my head in thought, there came a knock at the door.

"Stepfather? Stepmother? I'm here."

"Oh, Euphie?"

"Ah, you're already here. Good work, Anis."

Yes, it was Euphie who next entered my father's study, sitting down beside me with a smile. My parents were seated across the table facing us.

"...Euphie? Have you been working on something without telling me?" I asked.

She simply flashed me a bright smile. "No, we're still only at the discussion stage."

We had both been busy lately, sure, but what could she have done that needed my parents' approval?

"So? Father and Mother said you were going to explain something."

"Yes. As you've probably heard from Halphys, some of the prototype magical instruments are complete."

Incidentally, we had decided to call the musical instrument–type magical tools *magical instruments* for short, and I had indeed received a report noting that the prototypes were ready.

However, the craftsmen hadn't yet achieved their goal of manifesting spirits. Experimental results indicated that magical instruments had an amplification effect similar to magic wands, but being musical instruments, they weren't so easy to use and, as such, were naturally less effective than traditional wands.

On the other hand, their magic amplifying effect lasted the entire duration of the song and exerted an influence over a large area.

Nonetheless, they wouldn't do very much in actual service. There might yet be avenues to explore in future research, but at the moment, it was hard to call them particularly useful.

"As I reported to His Majesty, we've only taken our first step toward materializing spirits. However, it is a major accomplishment, so we've decided to hold a demonstration at an event in the near future to showcase our work."

"What?! So soon?!"

"There are several reasons for the urgency... The first is that the Ministry of the Arcane is under a lot of fire right now. The situation is becoming increasingly dire the more you mingle with the nobility at large."

"Huh?"

"Sounds like Grantz's doing...," my father murmured.

"He's as ruthless as ever... I sympathize," my mother added.

What on earth is Duke Grantz doing behind the scenes?!

While I sat there stunned, Euphie shot me a wry smile. "He still wants you to be queen one day, Anis. It's only natural that he would attempt to interfere."

"...Seriously?!"

"He knows what we both want, but that's beside the point. If I prove unworthy, they'll depose me without a second thought," she said, her eyes narrowing in a menacing grin.

Before I knew it, I realized that I was rubbing my arms as a chill coursed through my body.

My father and mother awkwardly averted their gazes. I similarly felt like avoiding reality.

"There's another reason, too. The later we hold the event to unveil the magical instruments, the less effective that demonstration will be. We want it to happen as soon as possible."

"…Is it running late?"

"Originally, I was hoping to have already held the demonstration quite some time ago."

"…It couldn't be held on schedule? What happened?" I asked, head cocked askew.

My mother frowned for some reason; my father looked uncomfortable as well.

Finally, he cleared his throat and interjected, "It isn't surprising if you forgot. It's been suspended for several years now."

"…What are you talking about?"

"Your birthday gala."

"…Huh?"

"Your *birthday*, silly girl! We stopped holding a celebration for it after you renounced your right to the throne and started acting like a hooligan!"

My mouth hung open in disbelief. It was true that large celebrations were commonplace for royal birthdays, and there had been several such events when I had been a child. But it had been years since any of that had taken place.

Right, it was no wonder that I had forgotten. My birthday had already passed, so it wasn't surprising that I hadn't even noticed it.

"But a birthday gala?! Why?!"

"The reason your birthday celebrations were called off was ostensibly that you had renounced your right to inherit the throne as well as your place in the royal family. However, if you trace it back to its root cause, you'll find it was the doing of the Ministry of the Arcane. So it would be beneficial to hold a gala to show the world how these two quarreling parties have since reconciled."

"I get what you're saying...but for my birthday...?"

"Holding an event now after such a long hiatus is also a good opportunity to show that you continue to be a member of the royal family," Euphie explained.

"This was a formal request from the Ministry of the Arcane," my father added, "but as your parent and as your king, it *would* be nice if we could hold something to make up for all the celebrations you've missed."

"...Isn't it a bit late for that, though?"

"We're doing this precisely because we've put it off for so long," Euphie continued. "This idea came from the Ministry of the Arcane itself—or more precisely, from Lang."

"Lang?"

"It's the most effective way to publicly declare that you and the ministry have made peace. By making up for all the missed celebrations, they will show wider society that they've come to acknowledge you."

"...Acknowledge me?"

"Yes. Even if the results are still somewhat weak, featuring the magical instruments there should still give them a boost," Euphie said. "So we would like to hold your birthday celebration as soon as possible."

"I could easily issue an order to make it happen... But I thought I would check with you first just in case, Anis," my father told me.

"There are so many reasons going for it that I don't see how you could say no."

Why did I feel like it was a little late for them to be asking my permission?

But that wasn't to say that I didn't want them to hold a celebration. I might have been the main party concerned here, but it didn't exactly feel that way.

"Then I'll assume your answer is yes," Euphie said. "Anis, could you leave the testing of the magical instruments to me and the Ministry of the Arcane?"

"Huh?"

"Halphys has been proactive with her advice from the very beginning, which is all the more reason why I thought it would be nice if you saw the results for yourself at the main event. In a way, the performance will be a gift to you from the Ministry of the Arcane."

"I see. Hmm, I did want to give the ministry credit for them anyway, so I guess I don't have any objection to letting them run with it... But doesn't that mean I won't have anything to do until that day?"

"What are you talking about, Anis?" my mother asked. "Now that the decision has been made, the date will be settled soon, too. And the number of available options is somewhat limited. In the meantime, you'll need to find a dress, and you might like to review your etiquette and manners."

"Huh?" I wrinkled my nose.

My mother's gaze instantly warmed. "Since it's been postponed all this time, we need to make sure everyone knows you're back to being a regular member of the royal family!"

Mother?!

Why were her eyes burning with such passion as she said that?! I felt like I was about to be scorched black from the heat. I glanced toward my father and Euphie for help, but they just looked away. My mother flashed me a broad grin.

"I'll be taking care of you for the next little while. Is that all right, Anis?"

"Eh?!"

"What do you say?"

"...Y-yes..."

Was my mother taking it upon herself to reeducate me? Would she be checking my manners all over again? And what was all that about getting a new dress? I was getting dizzy at what was about to befall me, and I wanted nothing more than to run away and hide.

"…It's been a long time, so let's give you a proper celebration."

"Why do I feel like I'm going to be scolded to death before any festivities, though?!"

"Oh? Are you admitting you're not up to it? Or are you itching to put your skills to use, Anis?" my mother asked, grinning from ear to ear.

"Anything I say here is just going to be used against me, isn't it?!" I cried back in a strained voice.

I thought this was going to be a celebration, but it sounded like I was going to go through hell before I got to have any fun!

It was totally unfair!

* * *

My mother stuck by my side like glue, checking on my manners and etiquette like a military training instructor, pushing me to the point of exhaustion to ensure I had a dress on time—when finally, I realized that it was the day of the gala. It had all happened so fast. To be perfectly honest, I still find it somewhat difficult to remember all of it.

The fact that my birthday was to be publicly celebrated for the first time in years meant that there were additional festive events taking place all through the castle town. Stalls lined the streets, and people were clamoring to drink and sing.

The royal parade moved through huge crowds of people. I was wearing a specially made dress and sitting beside Euphie as I waved to the onlookers.

Meanwhile, all those faces that had come to catch a glimpse were smiling and waving back.

"The crowds are as lively as ever," Euphie observed.

"That's just proof that the kingdom's prospering. So long as everything goes well today, I won't have any complaints."

"Yes, that's what matters most."

The two of us exchanged a few furtive words between lulls in the parade. The fact that everyone was making such a joyous commotion could only mean that all was well—for now at least.

I felt for the knights who had been dispatched to patrol the streets and maintain public order, although I hoped they would view defending this spectacle as a unique honor and give it their best efforts.

After this, there would be a birthday gala hosted by the Ministry of the Arcane. Indeed, if all went well, I would raise no objections. To be honest, I had been kept in the dark regarding most items on the agenda, so I had no idea what was going to happen there.

Filled with both anticipation and anxiety, I decided to focus on the task at hand—waving to the people milling around us.

* * *

Finally, once the parade was over, we took a short break to change our clothes and get ready.

Meanwhile, the sun had fallen, and night had begun. In the halls of the palace, various nobles were busy chatting among themselves.

Having become so familiar with this kind of scene in recent months, I caught my breath and entered alongside Euphie, bowing to the guests.

"Her Highness Princess Anisphia and Her Highness Princess Euphyllia have now arrived!"

As all eyes settled on us, the first faces that I spotted in the crowd belonged to Halphys and Marion.

They were appropriately dressed for the gala. I had to look twice at Halphys—well dressed as she was, she looked like a perfectly proper pretty young lady.

She ought to have been more confident, but she seemed nervous, not quite herself. Nonetheless, seeing her and Marion together, I thought they made a wonderful pair.

"Halphys! Marion!" I called out.

"Lady Euphyllia. Lady Anisphia. Good evening."

"Good evening to you, Halphys, Marion."

"Yes! Princess Anisphia! Congratulations again."

"Thank you. My birthday was actually a while ago now, though. And it's been a long time since I've celebrated it like this, so it's a little hard to relax."

"Thanks to you, the Ministry of the Arcane has been given a chance to redeem itself. And yet..." Marion stopped there.

"Indeed... I hope everything works out."

"Truly."

After this brief exchange, the two of them disappeared back into the crowd.

Next, various other individuals came to greet me in turn. I had been away from the social scene for a while, but I was finally starting to get the hang of it.

Granted, I wasn't quite as sure of myself as Euphie, the social butterfly by my side, carrying on a conversation as naturally and as fluid as running water. Meanwhile, I still had to let out a short chuckle every now and then to evade the occasional awkward question.

"Princess Anisphia, Princess Euphyllia," came a voice. "The Ministry of the Arcane, presiding over this ceremony, will soon be issuing a speech. Please make your way to the seats up on the stage."

"Huh? Is it already time? Right, got it."

"Shall we go, Anis?"

After a few more brief greetings, a butler arrived to guide us to the royal seats set up onstage at the front of the hall.

My heart began to pound at the thought that we were almost at the unveiling of the magical instruments. I only hoped that they would be received without any animosity...

"Hmm, here they come. Anis. Euphie," I heard my father say.

He and my mother were already seated up on the stage. Euphie and I sat down in the two remaining seats.

"Were you able to socialize properly, Anis?" my mother asked.

"Eh, well..."

"...Euphie?"

"Anis is still somewhat inexperienced, Stepmother, but practice will make perfect."

"…If you think so, Euphie, I suppose we can leave it at that."

My mother's question made my hair stand on end, but I managed to escape relatively unscathed. *Please, there's no need to pour all that pressure on me in the middle of a celebration!*

When I desperately averted my gaze, I noticed Lang making his way up onto the stage. Taking a position in the center, he glanced around at the gathered guests, cleared his throat, and spoke loud enough to be heard throughout the room:

"Your attention, please, everyone. Once again, we are gathered here today to celebrate the birthday of Her Highness Princess Anisphia. I, Lang Voltaire, shall serve as master of ceremonies tonight."

As Lang called out, the guests gathered throughout fell silent, their attention turning to us up on the stage.

"Congratulations again, Princess Anisphia," he continued. "We may have missed your actual birthday by several weeks, but I would like to thank you for trusting the Ministry of the Arcane to arrange this ceremony."

"…Your words are too generous for someone who has neglected their royal duties as I have," I answered, acutely aware of my mother's intense gaze fixed on me. "From this day on, I shall fulfill my responsibilities with a renewed sense of pride and awareness of my station. If not for the efforts of the Ministry of the Arcane, this opportunity would have been delayed until next year. Allow me to express my gratitude once again."

Only when I had finished speaking did the immense pressure emanating from my mother subside.

S-so I managed it?

"We will devote all our efforts to today's festivities in the hopes of providing you a worthy celebration… We shall begin by offering congratulatory speeches, followed by celebrating the anniversary of your birth with a blessing via spirit stones, as has been customary through ages past."

Lang's words were meant for the audience just as much as they were for us. Indeed, the entire room seemed to grow tense.

"However," he continued, "now that the magical tools that Your Highness so passionately advocated are meeting with widespread adoption, we have decided to review traditional rituals that consume large quantities of spirit stones. We at the Ministry of the Arcane have been entrusted by the realm with the sacred mission of inheriting our shared culture and tradition and passing it on to new generations. Culture must evolve to keep pace with changing times, but we mustn't allow change to sever our ties to tradition, so that we can relate to future generations how it is precisely the treasures of the past that have made the present moment possible."

He paused there for a moment to catch his breath, the guests gathered around displaying a wide range of reactions and responses.

"I hope that this event organized by the Ministry of the Arcane will become a new tradition linking past to present. Primordial light and darkness; the four essential elements of fire, earth, water, and wind; and the blessings of all the spirits that pervade this world are here with us. With this benediction, we celebrate the anniversary of the birth of Her Royal Highness Princess Anisphia and offer our sincerest prayers to the spirits around us. This is our blessing to you… Ensemble, you may enter!"

Having read aloud his congratulations, Lang issued a powerful declaration—and not a second later, the musicians carrying their instruments entered from the back of the other stage across the hall.

The instruments that the musicians brought in were all stringed, and what caught my attention most were the colors—they came in white, red, brown, blue, green, and black, each type of spirit represented by its own instrument.

"Today, I would like to dedicate a song to celebrate the birth of Her Highness Princess Anisphia using instruments made with the same processing technology as used for magical tools, to beseech the spirits for their blessings. Now then, everyone, if I may request your indulgence…"

Lang paused there, bowed—and then, looking up, exchanged a glance with the conductor at the head of the group of musicians.

The conductor, evidently having noticed the signal, offered him a slightly tense nod.

The lights in the hall dimmed, and the conductor raised his baton...

With that, the performance began.

The song was a common piece, often played when celebrating birthdays in the Kingdom of Palettia.

People and spirits had long lived together, hand in hand. The song was one of hope that the children of the realm would be blessed and protected, replete with wishes and prayers.

The musicians were impeccable, their performance flawless and pleasing to the ear. I listened on and squinted until I noticed Euphie, sitting by my side, slump down in her chair for a brief moment.

"Anis," she said, her voice slightly hoarse.

Just as I was thinking how unusual it was for her to speak up in the midst of a performance, something passed across the edge of my vision.

A dull shimmer was manifesting in the dim venue—six individual masses of pale light, wafting about, flickering in time with the music. Their shapes were still vague and undefined, the intensity of their light, of their presence, extremely tenuous.

But even so, they were unmistakably spirits.

Euphie squinted with joy, her lips curling in a smile as she watched the materializing spirits. She breathed an elated sigh. Perhaps because she was now a spirit covenantor, she felt something special at this strange sight.

The spirits flitting around, six trails of scintillating light, began to gather beside me—and the light began to fall like minute insect scales.

It was almost like they were sprinkling shards of light all over me. I held my breath at this fantastic sight, reaching out to scoop up the scales. Then, one after another, the light-clad spirits approached, drew up close as though to make physical contact, and then took off throughout the hall in apparent glee.

"Spirit stones are gifts from the spirits, and spirits are fragments of the world, mirrors that reflect the will of man," said Lang. "If you perform a wish, then the spirits will appear to you, answering your prayers... Without doubt, this is a most divine blessing—and one that *you* pointed out to us all."

"...It's incredible. They're beautiful," I whispered in admiration.

The other guests seemed to be having similar thoughts, and even in the dark, I could see that they were chasing the dancing spirits throughout the hall with their eyes.

The performance reached its climax, the music becoming increasingly passionate. When the finale sounded, the last chords lingered throughout the hall. Slowly, the sound faded, and with the end of the performance, the spirits, too, vanished from sight.

Eventually, someone remembered to start clapping—and at that moment, the entire venue erupted into a round of applause. I was similarly entranced, applauding the musicians for their performance.

Their duty was complete. The musicians, having been clearly on edge, bowed their heads. I had been busy watching the performance, noticing only now that Lang had approached the stage set aside for the royal family.

"Princess Anisphia," he called to me.

"Lang."

"...I offer you my congratulations on your birthday. May the spirits protect and bless you!" he said, falling to one knee and bowing.

Once more, there erupted from the audience another round of applause accompanied by cheers of support.

I watched on, speechless and in shock. All of a sudden, Euphie grabbed my hand, and my gaze turned from Lang to her.

The force of that movement sent tears streaming down my cheeks, though it took me a moment to recognize them for what they were. But here I was. Euphie looked at me as though watching a small child.

"...I've been blessed by this world, haven't I?" I asked. "By everyone who lives in this country, by the spirits we all rely on."

"Yes. All this time, you didn't want to be blessed because your research was regarded as heresy—but this blessing wouldn't have been possible without you, Anis," Euphie said, reaching out to wipe away my tears.

But still they wouldn't stop, streaming out drop after drop.

"You're blessed to be here, to be living in this world. Your life is very precious to us. So please, smile."

"...Mm-hmm."

My tears wouldn't cease, but that was okay. I let my emotions cascade down my cheeks, and I rose slowly from my seat.

"Lang...," I said, turning to him. "Thank you for your well-wishes. I am really, truly happy right now."

"...You're too generous."

He carefully got to his feet and offered me a gentle smile.

"...I still can't say whether magicology is the right path for the realm. But I have found one thing that I do believe in."

"...And what's that?"

"The futures we're both striving for aren't all that far apart. We're just taking different paths to get there. We all live to know happiness. I'm proceeding toward a joyous future through prayer to the spirits, and you're marching there by forging new possibilities. We may bump shoulders or block each other's way from time to time—but there's joy to be found in understanding one another, too, I think."

He placed a hand on his chest, bowed slightly, and declared, "I'm proud and overjoyed to have been present here today."

...Lang's words brought fresh tears to my eyes. As I shakily let out my breath, I extended a hand his way—and in response to that gesture, he glanced up with surprise.

"When two people make up, they shake hands," I told him. "Let's do that now as a sign of our continuing friendship."

"...Princess Anisphia."

"Do you mind if I help you lead the kingdom into the days ahead?"

*   *   *

Lang stared at my outstretched hand for a moment—then slowly reached out to take it in his own.

"I vow to learn with you, to march forward with you, and to defend the realm together with you, Your Highness."

His pledge brought a smile to my face. At that moment, a thunderous applause drummed through the hall.

Lang and I exchanged glances as the gathered guests cheered our blessing—and the two of us both broke out into fresh smiles.

* * *

"Good work today, Lang."

"...Is that you, Miguel?"

After completing the various ceremonies dedicated to Princess Anisphia, everyone in the hall went back to socializing among one another. There was a great deal of conversation, the guests abuzz with excitement, given everything that they had seen during the course of the evening.

All but skulking in a corner of the room with my back against the wall, I answered Miguel with a sniffle.

He had crept up on me without a sound and was now standing at the wall by my side as aloof as ever, clutching a wineglass in one hand.

"Are you relieved now to have received such heartfelt praise from the princess?" he asked.

"...Hmph."

"Hey, hey! I'm congratulating you here, you realize? This is great. The Ministry of the Arcane has managed to save face, no?"

"Let's just hope this excitement isn't a one-off thing."

"You can't be that oblivious, can you?" Miguel said with an exasperated sigh.

"...The performance of the magical instruments still wasn't quite good enough," I answered with a shrug. "We practiced again and again, but depending on the skill level of the individual musicians, at times we weren't able to summon the spirits at all. And the same musician isn't always able to call them, either. It's still a very unstable technology."

"Pulling all that off in such a short time frame is good enough, if you ask me."

"It's only thanks to Princess Anisphia's extensive research... I didn't do anything. These fruits are the result of her labors."

"You really are oblivious!" Miguel exclaimed in shock. His face, however, took on a strange cast.

I kept him in the corner of my vision until I spotted the person in question, Princess Anisphia, speaking with Princess Euphyllia.

"...Maybe the answer is surprisingly simple," I murmured.

"Huh?"

"I just thought if I had returned kindness with kindness...maybe we would have been able to forge stronger bonds earlier. That's it. It's all just hypothetical, really."

I'd overlooked her as an eccentric, ignorant child and had considered her a disgrace to the royal family.

Now, having come to believe that those views were unfounded prejudice, I was surprised by the change within myself.

It was true that I still felt some resistance to the theories she espoused, that I still rejected them at a certain level. But not so much that I wouldn't hear her out.

We were on different paths; that was undeniable. But we weren't staring out at entirely different destinations, either.

So perhaps we might one day find a road that we could walk together. Today at least, our trajectories seemed to have overlapped... It was rather difficult to find the words to express everything that had happened, though.

"...You might have had a different relationship? Still, all's well that ends well, right?"

"...I suppose so."

"Then it's good enough for now, huh? Anyway, congrats on a job well done," Miguel said, raising his wineglass.

I did the same, and the clink of our glasses meeting in a toast reverberated softly through the hall.

ENDING

A decent amount of time had passed since the success of my birthday gala, and in the meantime, we had pulled through one hectic day after another.

The Ministry of the Arcane, which had publicly declared its improved association with me, was reversing its many damaging rumors. But perhaps the biggest change of all was that the ministry had begun to ask me to give lectures of my own, similar to those that had been conducted through Duke Grantz's introductions.

Perhaps that was because, after the gala, I had begun to receive other invitations from the Ministry of the Arcane. Or perhaps it was because I had been publicly invited to the festivities with Euphie for the first time.

It went without saying, but the more invitations I received, the busier I found myself. At the same time, every day was fulfilling, and as they passed one after the next, my father summoned me, Euphie, Ilia, and Lainie to an audience.

We all gathered in his office, my mother and Duke Grantz already waiting there ahead of us. My father turned his gaze from outside the window—and as he glanced my way, I suddenly felt that things weren't quite right.

"You're here, Anisphia, Euphyllia."

"Father. What can we do for you today?"

"Hmm."

He nodded, then turned to my mother and Duke Grantz as though seeking confirmation. Looking closely, neither of them seemed their usual selves as they nodded quietly in response.

Seeing the three of them communicate without words, I felt like I had caught a pure glimpse of just how well they each understood one another.

"Euphyllia has been adopted into the royal family, and you've gone back to mingling with wider society, Anisphia," my father said. "To this day, the two of you have both been working toward the future of the kingdom, and you have gained the support of a great many nobles. Given all that, I think it's high time to pass my judgment."

"...Father, what are you—?"

"I'm thinking of abdicating."

Abdicating. My father's voice had risen with emotion at the word, but then he fell silent with an utterly placid calm. He spoke as though truly exhausted, a man finally trying to get some rest.

"The time is ripe. Even if I stay on the throne, there isn't much more I can do for the realm."

My back straightened as I hearkened these words. By my side, Euphie likewise stood up straight.

My father was abdicating. In other words, his task now was to decide who would follow him on the throne.

Euphie had been adopted into the royal family hoping to become queen, but whether or not she would actually sit on the throne depended on several factors. I had endeavored to do my best building social connections in case she didn't make it.

And now we would learn the result. Swallowing my breath, I awaited my father's decision.

"Succeeding me on the throne—will be you, Euphyllia."

I slowly let out my breath, releasing the tension that had built up inside me. At the same time, Euphie jumped slightly, bumping into my shoulder.

Flustered, I glanced her way, but she immediately straightened her posture. She closed her eyes once, took a deep breath, then looked back to my father.

"...Very well, Stepfather. I understand."

"You've done well thus far. There is a great deal of support for you to rule as the next queen, especially from the Ministry of the Arcane. But make no mistake—you haven't won this position because of Anis's boneheaded behavior. Rather, there are those who believe that she should have the freedom to forge a bright future for us all while you handle the responsibilities of queen. Never forget that you have been chosen as the symbol of the realm, to serve as its ruler and lead it for the betterment of its people."

"Yes. I will take your admonition to heart."

"Anis. From now on, you will support Euphyllia as the queen's sister. She believes in your ideals more than anyone else, so be sure never to betray her. Push forward together into the future, the both of you."

"Yes, Father. My future is with Euphie."

Staring straight at the two of us, my father nodded, then closed his eyes. Finally, he knelt down before us.

We were taken aback by this sudden action. For my father, the king, to kneel before anyone—ordinarily, that would have been unimaginable.

"Anisphia. Euphyllia. I'm sorry. I've been an unworthy king. All I've left for your generation are problems, so many of them. If things had gone the way they should have, I would never have been king. And now I'm passing the burden onto you."

"Father! Please, don't say that!"

"No. Just once, let me apologize from the bottom of my heart. I took the throne after defeating my brother, brought up to be king. I smote him because I was afraid he would tear the country apart, that its people and territory would be destroyed by war. I'm a coward. I was neither a man of valor nor a true king. I was only ever a powerless figurehead. If not for Sylphine and Grantz, my life would have been forfeit long ago."

My father bowed his head, his shoulders convulsing as he offered this confession.

"Despite all of that, I've been striving to accomplish what I was supposed to do... But the more I see you both, the more I realize how much I lacked talent like yours. If only I did. People see me as a gentle, peace-loving king, but in the end, I've been simply powerless. From the very beginning, no one expected me to take the throne. Which was only natural."

My father's words were too heartbreaking. My mother and Duke Grantz both looked downcast, neither saying anything. It would have been easy to refute him. There were so many positives that had come from my father's rule.

However, looking at the way that things were now, it was hard to say that he had excelled in the role. He had lost Allie, his son and heir, and his own vassals had been plotting against him. Nor could we say that the problems inherited from his own father's generation had been resolved.

"Ruling a kingdom, navigating politics—these aren't things you can do with kindness alone. Sometimes, sacrifices are necessary to protect the realm. You can't shift that responsibility onto anyone else. That, I believe, is what it means to be king. And that's why I was unable to fulfill my duties."

"Father..."

"Don't be like me, Euphyllia. No, I don't need to tell you that, do I? You're much better suited to rule than I ever was... But don't fool yourself into thinking that's the only thing you need."

My father spoke calmly, slowly rising to his feet and placing a hand on Euphie's shoulder.

"It shames me to say this, but I was nothing more than a king. And that alone isn't good enough. All I could do was hand over the mantle to Anisphia and Algard, to force them to one day take the reins. I failed to teach them anything else. As a parent, I'm ashamed."

"...You don't need to blame yourself, Your Majesty," Euphie said.

"Then do you have respect for me? Do you approve of everything I've done?"

"...Of course I do."

"That was a mean-spirited question. Thank you for your consolation, but that isn't quite enough," my father said with a gentle smile. "It's difficult to balance being both a ruler and an individual. The responsibilities that fall on your shoulders are far from light, you understand? But if you abandon them, what awaits is stagnation, a future in which nothing moves forward. You probably already know all this, but let me state it outright, Euphyllia. Now that you have become a spirit covenantor, you must never forget this. You must be yourself. That's what I hope for you."

"...Stepfather."

"Anisphia. You more than anyone ought to understand how difficult it is to be both royalty and individual. So stand by Euphyllia's side and support her."

"...Yes. Of course I will, Father."

"...And don't feel like having others offer you their protection is a burden. You might feel embarrassed at times, and you won't want to hurt those you care about. That's important. But don't get caught up in those emotions. Put them aside when you must. Even I can say that much, thanks to having such a fine wife and a loyal friend."

With that, he placed his free hand on my shoulder and flashed me a mischievous smile before looking up at my mother and Duke Grantz.

"...I should have said all this sooner," he began. "If I had, maybe Algard would still be here. Then again, perhaps it takes more than words to nurture this seed. It's difficult, isn't it?"

"...But surely you have more than just regrets?" Euphie asked.

"Ah, that's right. Never forget your regrets, but don't forget to keep moving forward, either. I can't say I was really able to put that lesson into practice, so I'll leave it to you both now. After I step down from the throne, I shall spend the remainder of my days serving as a foundation for you both to build on. I hope the future you lead us into will be like the lightest of wings."

With that, he brought Euphie and me together by the shoulders in a warm embrace. Then, after patting us on the back a few times, he slowly pulled away.

"I'll leave the rest to you two," he said.

Yes, I heard my voice say in unison with Euphie's. With a final nod, my father turned next to Duke Grantz.

"Grantz, as your king, I command you—if you have anything to say to Euphyllia as her father, don't hold back."

"...Your Majesty."

"Or as your friend, do I have to tell you to face your own daughter without shying away? I hope you won't have the same regrets I do."

"...Your concerns are unnecessary," Duke Grantz, vassal and friend, said with an exasperated sigh as he approached Euphie.

Father and daughter looked at each other in silence for a moment. "Euphyllia," Duke Grantz said at last. "You are quite similar to me, which is why I cannot admire those parts of you that are not worthy of praise. I suppose we're alike in those areas."

"...I'm not as bad-natured as you, though, am I, Father?"

"Hmm. Maybe not. But don't try to deny that you have your foibles. You are inflexible, especially when it comes to Princess Anisphia."

"...That's nobody's business."

"Isn't it a parent's responsibility to make it their business? There are limits, yes, but I suppose we didn't try hard enough. Or maybe we only looked out for you in the literal sense. If that's why you only walked in my shadow while betrothed to Prince Algard, I have no excuse to offer."

"...Father."

"I'm prouder of you now that you're willing to face me head-on. You don't need to feel trapped in my shadow anymore. Use your parents as a springboard and keep pushing forward," Duke Grantz said, patting her on the head. His expression at that moment was the most human, fatherly look that I had ever seen him wear. "You've grown, Euphyllia," he finished.

"..."

Euphie's breath trembled, and she stiffened slightly. As she moved to rest her forehead against her father's chest, Duke Grantz calmly wrapped his arms around her in a hug.

The two remained that way for a long moment before pulling back as though nothing had happened. There was no lingering feeling, but still I was left with the impression that they each seemed satisfied by this exchange.

"Anis…Euphie…"

"Mother."

"I'm the one who was most absent from your lives, and I'll always regret not being there for you. It's not about offering or accepting forgiveness. I just can't forgive myself."

No, I was about to say but stopped myself. Even though she looked sad, my mother was smiling as she took my hand and Euphie's and pulled us close.

"I wish I could have been a better mother for you to remember me by," she said. "I wish I could have made more memories with you and shared in that joy together…"

"…We're going to make plenty more from now on," Euphie told her.

"Yes. But even if we can make more, they can't replace those that never were. It's not a simple exchange. So no matter how many more wonderful memories we make, I'll always have regrets, and that's something that will haunt me forever," my mother declared as though in prayer as she gripped our hands.

"…Yes."

"You both have wonderful sets of wings on your backs. Nothing can stop you from flying far into the future. So take off without regrets. If you get tired, rest. But don't be afraid to fly, and don't look down with remorse. You are our pride and joy."

Our pride and joy. When I heard those words, my vision began to blur as tears welled up in my eyes. Desperately trying to hold myself together, I smiled back at her and said, "Please watch over us, so we can fly as far as we can go."

"Of course. I'll always be watching over you."

My mother released our hands and patted us both on the shoulder, holding me and Euphie in her arms as she fixed us with a smile, her cheeks streaked with tears.

My father and Duke Grantz watched on calmly, both of them seemingly staring somewhere far into the distance.

Only then did I understand. Until now, they had both stood ahead of us, as king and duke, as parents. But now, I realized, we had moved forward.

So I poured all my strength into my legs and stood up straight. I couldn't let them see me slouching now. I wanted to live up to their expectations, so that they couldn't possibly be ashamed of me.

"Thank you," I said. "For everything."

From now on, I wouldn't let them carry the burden alone. Awash with fresh determination and gratitude, I offered them my heartfelt thanks.

* * *

A formal proclamation was issued that my father had officially nominated Euphie as the kingdom's next ruler, and shortly thereafter, her coronation ceremony was set to take place.

Since my father and the others had already discussed it all with us beforehand, the preparations proceeded without much hassle or fuss. During this time, I checked in with Halphys and Garkie to see how everyone had responded to news of Euphie's accession to the throne.

"Well, they all thought it would be her," Garkie said.

"Yes. I wouldn't say they're negative toward you, Lady Anisphia—rather, they seem to think it better that you continue to advocate for magicology," Halphys added.

"You and Lady Euphyllia get along pretty well, so as long as there's no friction, I don't think people will have any problem accepting that she's more suited to the job," Garkie opined.

Apparently, that's how it was. It seemed that Euphie's accession was being welcomed without any major backlash.

I was happy that everything had turned out the way I had hoped. However, it was strange to think how my position would change from here on out, and so I passed the days restless as I prepared for the coronation ceremony.

But time waits for no one, and the day arrived in the blink of an eye. Like that, I found myself being outfitted by Ilia in a suitable dress.

"...You're very quiet today," she said.

"Even someone like me is bound to get a little anxious on a day like this," I replied.

"Indeed. I'm glad to hear you're reacting appropriately."

"...Do you *actually* think that?" I asked, glaring resentfully at her in the mirror.

Ilia, however, stared back at me with a guiltless look. "Your hair has grown out a little," she commented.

"Oh? I haven't got it cut lately, now that you mention it."

"You're a little taller, too."

"Really?!"

"I would say Euphyllia has grown more, though."

"Why do you raise me up just to throw me back down?"

Euphie was certainly getting taller. But she would stop growing soon, right? I didn't like the idea of us being too different in height.

"Don't worry—you're growing nicely, too, Lady Anisphia."

"...Mm-hm."

"Congratulations again. I hope to continue serving you by your side into the future."

"...You'll upset Lainie, talking like that."

"She's rather cute when she sulks."

Lainie wasn't with us as she was busy helping Euphie get ready. No doubt things weren't exactly simple over on their end, either.

At that moment, there came a knock at the door, followed by my mother entering the room.

"Anis, are you ready?" she asked.

"Yes, Mother. As you can see, I'm finished."

"...You're acting very grown up today, don't you think?"

"Why are you and Ilia both disparaging me?"

"Because we practically have a daily routine, no? You're always complaining about how heavy your dresses are and how difficult they are to move around in," she said with a stern look, though she quickly relaxed her gaze and flashed me a grin. "Well…we're not exactly in a position to criticize others, I suppose."

"*We?*"

"I don't particularly like dresses, either, you know? As a girl, I thought wielding a spear was the best thing in the whole wide world. Even your father said he would rather wear light clothing and tinker in the soil and dirt than wear a stiff nobleman's outfit. And then you ended up so like us both…"

"…Mother."

"No, I ought to say my part. I regret it all—really I do. I wish I had done so much better for you. There's no end to the things I could have done differently."

My mother, sapped of energy, shook her head and looked up as though to free herself from those negative emotions. "Anis, today is going to mark an end for you. But it's also a new beginning."

"Yes."

"You should live your life the way you want. I might be here to nag you, but you're free to decide for yourself whether to take my advice or not."

She leaned in just close enough so as not to ruin my makeup or dress. I, too, placed a hand on her shoulder, leaning her way. After a few warm moments, we both took a step back.

"Now, we should be off. We need to be there to welcome your father and Euphyllia."

"Right, Mother. Let's go."

"…I thought you might need more of a push. But now you're inviting *me* to join *you*, I see," she said, staring up at me tearfully.

But before any tears could fall, she wiped them away with her fingers and joined me to walk side by side to the venue.

The coronation hall was already filled with nobles in advance of the ceremony, each of them sitting on the edge of their seat waiting for the event to get underway.

When my name and my mother's were called out, all eyes turned to us. I could spot more than a few familiar faces among the crowd.

Tilty—whom I would never have expected to show her face at an event like this—was standing there looking listless. When her eyes met mine, she shrugged and smiled uncomfortably.

Halphys was next to Marion, offering me a friendly glance—and that was enough to bring me joy.

I spotted Garkie among the knights defending the hall, and he, too, flashed me a mischievous grin.

Also with the knights was, of course, Commander Sprout of the Royal Guard. As he turned toward me and my mother, he offered us both a friendly nod.

I also spotted Lang and Miguel, and various nobles with whom I had exchanged words during my magicology lectures and at evening parties. Next were Duke Grantz and Duchess Nerschell, the closest to royalty of anyone in the room.

Duchess Nerschell gave us a small, inconspicuous wave. She glanced at her husband, sitting there without saying anything, out of the corner of her eyes, and almost let out a derisive snort.

…That was when I remembered Allie, who by rights should have been standing among us. I stared at the ground for a moment, before straightening my back once again.

My mother and I made our way through the crowd of familiar faces and took our seats in the area designated for the royal family.

There, the elderly man who would be presiding over the ceremony was waiting for us with a gentle smile—Acting Director Graphite of the Ministry of the Arcane. It was only natural that the most senior official would preside over a royal coronation. He was apparently Miguel's grandfather, but his nondescript elderly appearance didn't leave much of a lasting impression.

"I've been waiting for you, Queen Sylphine, Princess Anisphia. I'm so pleased to see you on this most auspicious of days. Now, I would like to begin the coronation ceremony. Everyone, if you could please be silent."

The room became quiet as the master of ceremonies bellowed his order. Then, after a short pause, one of the knights guarding the entrance called out, "His Majesty King Orphans and Her Highness Princess Euphyllia have arrived!"

The announcement echoed throughout the hall until silence once again prevailed. The first figure to appear was my father, dressed in an outfit even more splendid and regal than usual, his head adorned by a crown handed down through generations. It was an incredibly important artifact, brought out only for only special ceremonies like this.

Euphie was close behind, clad in the most beautiful dress that I had ever seen—the design was both artful and stylish.

Most of her dresses were designed to accentuate her femininity. Today's, however, served to give off an abundantly regal impression.

She strode with a confident posture, and her self-assurance made you want to attend to her yourself. You could feel her determination to serve as the kingdom's next ruler. Utterly captivated, I watched as she and my father stepped up to the stage, where my mother and I were waiting.

"King Orphans, Your Majesty. Princess Euphyllia, Your Highness," said Acting Director Graphite.

"I'm sorry, Graphite. Making you wait up here in your old age."

"Ho-ho-ho. I never imagined that I, who witnessed your ascension to the throne, would still be here to see your abdication. Fate is an inscrutable thing indeed."

The acting director gazed at my father with a smile that could only be described as that of an affectionate elderly grandfather. The fact that he used to serve as director of the Ministry of the Arcane himself probably meant that he had presided over my father's coronation as well. It was only natural to find it a curious turn of fate that he would be entrusted with the same ruler's abdication long after his retirement.

"Then let us begin. Your Majesty, King Orphans Il Palettia—we, your retainers, are so very pleased to welcome you on this auspicious day."

The assembled nobles in the hall each bowed their heads to this solemn proclamation.

"O King who has guided us, we beseech you to speak."

"Hmm."

My father nodded once, then turned to the mass of bowing nobles. Taking a deep breath, he closed his eyes to concentrate all his thoughts into that transitory moment. Then, after slowly opening them, he spoke up. "Many years have passed since I ascended to the throne. I'm sure a great many of you remember it. At the time, the realm was in turmoil. It would be no exaggeration to say that the Kingdom of Palettia was on the verge of destruction."

His voice was solemn, grave—replete with regret that couldn't be concealed.

Originally, my father wasn't in a position to accede to the throne. Fate had placed him there. My heart ached to think of the hardships he had been forced to endure to become king. He, who had wanted no more than to indulge in his hobby of tinkering in the soil, had ended up becoming the pinnacle of the realm's political sphere.

"It's thanks to all those vassals who have supported me that I'm here today. It's my greatest treasure and honor to have served as your king. However, I do have regrets. My achievements as sovereign are far too few. I doubt I've done enough to earn the honor you all bestow upon me."

My father paused there, silence engulfing the room.

"...Everyone, please raise your heads," he called out, and one by one those assembled started looking up.

"As of this day, I, Orphans Il Palettia, am stepping down from my position as king. I ask you, my subjects who have supported me throughout my reign, to heed my words and accept this call: I nominate Princess Euphyllia Fez Palettia as our next ruler."

At last, my father came out with his pronouncement. The room grew suddenly tense, no one willing to so much as exhale out of fear of breaking the silence.

"What I can say with pride is that I've left a legacy for the future, a seed to be nurtured. I shall place Euphyllia on the throne as our queen, while Anisphia will support her. I ask you all to offer them your blessings! These children will open the path to the future for the entire realm! And so I hereby hand over the throne to one who is more worthy than I!"

…Like an explosion bursting out, the hall erupted into a thunderous outcry of cheers and applause.

This continued for a long moment—then, as though to quiet down the assembled nobles, my father raised his hand. The room fell suddenly silent.

"Euphyllia," he called out. "Step forward."

"Yes," Euphie replied, doing as instructed. She glanced up at him for a moment before kneeling.

"I ask of you: Should I appoint you as queen, are you ready to take on the burden of that responsibility?"

"I swear by the spirits to shoulder this great charge."

My father nodded—and all that was left was to place the crown atop her head and her accession to the throne would be undeniably affirmed.

"Anisphia," my father called.

"Eh? Ah, um, yes!"

All of a sudden, my name came up, and I hurried to respond. But why on earth was he addressing *me*?

Ignoring my evident confusion, my father removed his crown and held it out to me.

"*You* should be the one to crown her."

"…Me?"

But I had never heard of this procedure before. Huh? Wasn't the usual custom for one king to hand the crown directly to the next ruler?

"Euphie is not a direct descendant of the royal family. She will be taking over the responsibilities that should have been ours to bear. You must entrust them to her so that she never forgets their weight."

My heart pounded at my father's words. I swallowed deeply, staring down at the crown in his outstretched hands.

I—who by every right should have worn that crown myself—was now bestowing it on Euphie. There was certainly something to be said for this most intentional of displays.

And I recognized once more that I was handing her a heavy responsibility as queen.

"...I understand."

I took a deep breath before accepting the crown from my father. By itself, it wasn't particularly heavy—yet it felt impossibly so.

My father took a step back, allowing me to stand before Euphie in his place. The next moment, she knelt down, looking up at me.

"Anis."

"Euphie."

Both of us spoke so quietly that even in that silent hall, no one could possibly have heard us.

I was about to place the weight of the entire kingdom on her shoulders—to the one person who believed in my dreams more than anyone else. To her, I was about to offer this unimaginably heavy duty.

"I swear I'll never let you bear this crown alone, Euphie."

I would never forget the weight of the responsibility that I was giving to her. That's why I would always be there for her, as her strongest supporter. We would pursue our dreams in unison.

From here on out, we would be together, no matter what. I would keep this promise for the rest of my life.

"Anis," Euphie called once more—this time with a note of affection. "Am I worthy of your honor?" she asked.

I had no answer to that question. Instead, I felt tears welling up in my eyes, so much so that they threatened to blur everything before me.

When I first met her, she was so fragile and wounded that I feared she might break apart at the slightest nudge.

She was suffering, struggling, unable to find a way out, and she told me how she wanted to support my dreams. You could probably even say that I saved her.

But she saved me, too. She gave me the salvation that I was too afraid to take for myself.

                              *   *   *

And I loved her so much now.

My thoughts were overflowing without end. And finally we had
arrived here. Of course, this wasn't the end. You might even say that
it was a new beginning. But there was most certainly a path that had
brought us to this point.

The weight in my hands was made up of all these feelings and thoughts.
That was why it was so heavy. It was painful; it made me want to cry and
toss it aside. But it was so important that I didn't let go.

I loved her. I loved the time that we had spent together and the future
that we were heading toward. And I wanted to honor everything about
this person who loved me more than anything else.

"Honor alone isn't enough. I want to give you so much more. I want
to experience everything with you, Euphie."

So let's carry this together as we walk the path you've chosen.

I gently placed the crown that Euphie desired atop her head. She
dipped her head slightly as she accepted it.

Now that she was crowned, she slowly rose to her feet and cast her gaze
first to my father and then to my mother.

My father offered a serene smile and nodded in satisfaction. My
mother wiped away tears of joy.

"Congratulations, Euphyllia."

"Thank you, Stepfather, Stepmother."

"…Now, show everyone what you look like."

At my father's urging, Euphie nodded and turned around to face
the hall.

At the same moment, Acting Director Graphite announced, "I hereby
proclaim your accession to the throne! Her Majesty Queen Euphyllia
Fez Palettia! May the spirits bless our new sovereign!"

Chanting filled the hall as the guests prayed to the spirits, followed by
decisive applause.

Everyone was focused on Euphie, now accepted as ruler. A spirit covenanter, the successor to an almost legendary process passed down through the ages, had now written her name into the history books.

Today was without doubt a turning point for the ages. The excitement of standing witness to this moment must have been fueling everyone's enthusiasm, as the applause and cheers continued without end.

"Silence! Her Majesty Queen Euphyllia will now address her vassals!" A deep voice calmed the audience's buzzing.

That fervor, however, continued to linger under the surface—every last person in the room turned to Euphie so as not to miss her next words.

Then, glancing over the hall, she placed a hand on her chest and spoke in a clear, rich voice. "I'm proud to stand before you on this auspicious day. As you know, I am not an immediate descendent of the royal family, but rather I was permitted to join it after entering into a spirit covenant."

Partly in prayer, partly an expression of her innermost wishes, she puffed out her chest as she continued to speak. "But there is something I must ask you all not to forget. We have inherited the miracle of magic from the first sovereign who founded our Kingdom of Palettia, and we have protected that realm by entrusting the nobility with the honor and responsibility of wielding magic. The weight of that history continues to bequeath us with a sense of pride even today. However, these long-standing traditions have brought about a disconnect between those of us who can use magic and those who cannot, which has in turn undermined the entire nation. It has also brought about untold grief."

The first thing that floated to my mind was Allie. And then there was the coup d'état that forced my father to take revenge on his own brother. The root cause behind all of it was this disconnect, ensuring friction between the nobility and the common folk.

A people oppressed by corrupt aristocrats, filled with resentment and fury. Nobles who had inherited magical talents through blood alone. It had already brought about so many tragedies.

"Once again, we must return to these essential questions: What is magic? What should the nobility be? What is the right path for our nation? I will do my utmost to lead the way down the road that I believe to be right. This is not a revival of ancient legends, nor a restoration to that which existed in ages past. My pledge to you is a symbol—one of the inheritance of tradition, but also of rebirth."

The realm was rotten. She had basically just said so aloud. But she wasn't about to give up on it. If necessary, she would nurture new buds to revitalize it. And so she pledged to us all now.

"The times are changing, and the role of the nobility must likewise evolve. I will not tell you to abandon those things that have given you such pride. But I ask that you don't reject change. I strongly believe that this new wind picking up in our kingdom is a sign of good fortune! And the person who convinced me of this—is Anisphia Wynn Palettia!"

After calling out my name, Euphie approached by my side, tugging at my hand until we stood shoulder to shoulder.

I was almost taken aback by her sudden embrace, but before I could react, she continued, "Anis showed me a new future, one of unparalleled potential. But I understand your fear of the unknown. There is nothing more terrifying than traveling without knowing where you might end up. The future that Anis is building may seem to us dark, with no lamp-posts to guide the way. But it isn't all darkness! It's no different than the night sky—filled with the sparkling of the stars above! It is not a path devoid of light! The light is in ourselves—in each and every one of us!"

Euphie appealed to the crowded hall, her speech so strong and passionate that it consumed the entire space. Then her voice took on further emotion. "I saw the light. And when I did, I knew that I, too, could shine."

She turned her gaze toward me, grabbed me by the shoulders, and shifted position so that we were facing each other head-on.

And then she kissed me.

I froze up. A gasp erupted from the audience. The ensuing silence was so deep that I could even hear my own heart pounding in my chest.

"I love you with all my heart, more than anyone else. You are my light."

"Eu...phie..."

"I will show you all this light, together with the person I love most! I will show this kingdom hope! Possibilities! I hereby swear to the Primordials and the Four Great Elements! With this declaration of love, I will bring prosperity to Palettia! Please join us for the dawn of a new era!"

Everyone must have been taken aback by the sheer suddenness of what had just happened. But after a short pause, someone began clapping—and then applause echoed through the audience like a rising wave. Small cheers gave way to thunderous cries of support, until the loudest ovation of the day filled the room.

I stood there trembling. To think she had kissed me, here of all places, and then confessed her love...! N-not only that, but she had sworn an oath to the spirits, s-saying how much she loved me...!

My father had one hand against his forehead in exasperation, but my mother was wearing an indescribable smile.

Left with no clue whatsoever how to respond to all this, I stared at Euphie as my face turned red.

Before I knew it, she wrapped her arms around my waist, leaving me no room to escape. I found myself almost hating the loving look that she so dazzled me with.

"...You've...done a hell of thing there...!" I said.

"I wanted to keep you in check," she replied.

"*That's* why you kissed me in front of everyone?!"

The cheers continued echoing throughout the room, so the audience couldn't possibly have overheard our argument—but even so, we kept our voices low.

Euphie, meanwhile, seemed to have heard me just fine. Her eyes narrowed in a soft frown—her expression so petulant that it made me want to slap her across the cheek.

"You can slap me if you want, but I won't let you stop me."

"U-ugh...! Euphie, y-you idiot...!"

I can't hold my face up anymore!

My only hope was that this whole situation would reach its conclusion as soon as possible.

* * *

Night had fallen, the coronation ceremony now behind us.

In the moonlit room, I was sitting atop my bed like a threatening animal. Euphie, at the receiving end of this intimidating look, simply smiled awkwardly at me.

"It's about time you cheered up, Anis."

"...After what you did to me?"

"Which is why I'm apologizing now. I should have at least told you what I was planning beforehand."

"...That's not what I mean."

"...Then why are you so upset?" she muttered, perplexed.

I'm just as perplexed!

I puffed out my cheeks, holding tightly on to the pillow in my arms.

"...You're so unfair."

"Unfair?"

"...You're *always* unfair."

She really was. How could she not be, using a kiss to keep me quiet in a place like that, while everyone was watching during something so important?

It wouldn't be easy for anyone to try to get her to choose a royal consort after that display, though. She had said explicitly that she loved me, as much as anyone could.

"You *are* unfair."

I mean, I loved her, too—but the way she kept acting in front of others, she made it look so one-sided.

I laid the pillow down beside me and drew closer to her, then placed my hands on her shoulders and pressed my lips firmly to hers.

We had kissed so many times—but never before had I taken the initiative myself, and I saw her eyes snap open in surprise. It was such a good feeling.

"I love you," I said. "I love everything about you—I would give up everything for you."

There, even though it almost made me want to cry, I had clearly put my feelings into words. I forced a smile.

Today was the happiest that I had felt in my whole life, and I wanted to know even greater joy. It was all Euphie's fault that I had ended up like this. I couldn't handle it anymore, not by myself.

"...Fine," I said.

"...Anis?"

"Just for today, I'll let you do anything you want to me."

I hoped it was a good thing that my voice was shaking at least. I averted my gaze, so I couldn't see her reaction. Nonetheless, she remained frozen in place for a short moment before reaching out.

"Are you sure...?" she asked.

"...If you keep asking again and again, I might change my mind."

It was a quiet night. We were facing each other so close that we could even hear one another breathing.

We were both sitting on the bed in our nightgowns, but we were clearly ill at ease. We had slept together countless times already, so it shouldn't have been something to feel embarrassed about. But even so, my heart was beating faster than usual. Yes, there was something slightly different about this night.

Ever since Euphie had become a spirit covenantor, replenishing her magical energy from me had been her main form of sustenance. So in a way, my magical energy was the best treat of all.

There were various ways to ingest magical energy. For example, you could do so by consuming bodily fluids such as blood or through physical contact.

In the end, it was just skin-to-skin contact—and yet, it was *skin-to-skin contact.* Our relationship had changed to one between lovers, but I had never before let it go so far.

To be honest, I hadn't been able to take the plunge. I was afraid that I might drown in my own joy. But now I had hopefully come to terms with my emotions.

Maybe today's milestone had marked a turning point. Euphie had expressed her love for me, and perhaps that had helped me get a better handle on my own feelings.

But maybe it really was all right for me to do this? I felt now that I could give her my all.

"...I can feel something welling up inside me again hearing you say that," Euphie said as she caressed my ear with her outstretched hand.

A tingling sensation coursed down my spine as her fingers traced from my earlobe all the way to my hairline.

"I always thought this day would come. But now that it's here...I don't know what to say."

She let out a chuckle, looking truly happy. Ever since she'd come to live here in the detached palace, her expressions had softened; she was so relaxed now that she hardly even resembled her earlier self.

...Ah, so this was how much she liked me...

"...Shame, willpower—I've had to weigh the balance between a lot of things lately, so if you keep praising me too much, I might go berserk," I said.

"Yes, I know. All the more reason, Anis."

She paused there, tracing her finger from my ear down to under my chin, to gently lift my head. Her kisses continued soundlessly.

I closed my eyes, accepting her lips as I tried to calm my body, which was growing tenser by the second.

There was a pause in that sweet onrush of kisses. I heard her call out my name in a gentle voice, causing my brain to go numb.

"...Ngh, I can't wait any longer," she breathed in a frenzy, her voice so hot and buoyant that it almost burned me.

Her hand fell over my shoulder, followed by the weight of her body.

Before I knew it, I was lying on my back looking up at her, her silvery hair draping around my face like a curtain.

All that we could make out were each other's faces. Her cheeks were so flushed that I could discern their red tinge just by the wan light of the moon; her eyes looked to be melting, as though their depths hid an impossible heat.

Her attitude and behavior were completely different than usual. I was left stunned. My chest panged as though caught in a vise.

Euphie, normally so composed and perfect, was now seeking me out, all of me. All at once, I was happy, embarrassed, I felt like crying—and I realized that I could offer her the most natural of smiles.

Maybe she took that expression as a sign to keep going, as her kisses that followed were so rough that they were more like bites.

And she's normally so ladylike...

When finally she released me, it took all that I had just to catch my breath. Seeing that she had pushed me to the very brink, she flashed me a small smile—one so unusual and provocative that it sent a shiver down my spine.

"We might not have any time to sleep tonight," she said.

"...Don't break me, all right?" I pleaded, my mouth twitching slightly.

Euphie didn't reply with words—she simply smiled as her lips closed on mine all over again.

Will I really have a chance to catch my breath today? I wondered as I wrapped my arms around Euphie's back and she mercilessly tried to drown me.

AFTERWORD

Piero Karasu here. Thank you so much for reading the fourth volume of *The Magical Revolution of the Reincarnated Princess and the Genius Young Lady*. I'm so happy to have been able to deliver this latest installment of the tale to you all.

This volume picks up from the last one and marks the beginning of a new life for Anis while at the same time being the sum effect of all her trials and successes thus far.

In the third volume, Anis and Euphie set out to embrace new changes while inheriting the fate brought to them through the ages. This time, we follow the two as they work to forward that goal, and we begin to see how the consequences of their actions begin to ripple through society.

We see the first steps toward change in the appearance of Halphys and Gark, both influenced by Anis's dreams and ideals and intent on walking a new path, and in Lang, who was formerly at odds with her.

These may be big changes in the broader systems that govern the kingdom, but as the social milieu and environment shift, so, too, do the people—and that's when we find a shift in the relationship between Ilia and Lainie.

For many years, the Kingdom of Palettia had remained stagnant because of its deeply ingrained values. The warped nature that it developed was corruption in the truest meaning of the word, but at long last, it is finally being corrected and resolved.

All of this leads to Euphie's accession to the throne, to our heroines both being entrusted with bearing the weight of the responsibilities inherited from their parents' generation into their various newfound positions.

As the author of this work, I wish for nothing more than to help you, the reader, experience the same hope and expectation for the future that these two girls will one day build.

Speaking of happiness and hope, I'm overjoyed to hear that the manga adaptation by Harutsugu Nadaka is doing so well! Her power of expression has helped broaden the world of the narrative to even greater levels, enough to prompt even those who have already read the light novels to gasp in surprise! If you haven't picked up a copy yet, please do! Thank you!

It's only thanks to the support I've received from so many areas that I've been able to bring this fourth volume of the tale to you. I would like to show my appreciation to my illustrator, Yuri Kisaragi, and to my editor for all their support—thank you both so much for helping me make it this far!

I'll close this afterword with a wish: May the circle of change that has started unfolding in the story continue to expand. Until next time.

PIERO KARASU

HAVE YOU BEEN TURNED ON TO LIGHT NOVELS YET?

86—EIGHTY-SIX, VOL. 1-11

In truth, there is no such thing as a bloodless war. Beyond the fortified walls protecting the eighty-five Republic Sectors lies the "nonexistent" Eighty-Sixth Sector. The young men and women of this forsaken land are branded the Eighty-Six and, stripped of their humanity, pilot "unmanned" weapons into battle...

Manga adaptation available now!

WOLF & PARCHMENT, VOL. 1-6

The young man Col dreams of one day joining the holy clergy and departs on a journey from the bathhouse, Spice and Wolf. Winfiel Kingdom's prince has invited him to help correct the sins of the Church. But as his travels begin, Col discovers in his luggage a young girl with a wolf's ears and tail named Myuri, who stowed away for the ride!

Manga adaptation available now!

SOLO LEVELING, VOL. 1-7

E-rank hunter Jinwoo Sung has no money, no talent, and no prospects to speak of—and apparently, no luck, either! When he enters a hidden double dungeon one fateful day, he's abandoned by his party and left to die at the hands of some of the most horrific monsters he's ever encountered.

Comic adaptation available now!